June 8

Dear Miss Eula,

Well, you are gone. I hope you are happy. I am not.

For your information, Melba Jane is still here. I am working on a disappearing potion to make her vanish.

Mama is in the kitchen, cooking, cooking, cooking. She is still writing about zucchini, so I know what <u>we</u> are having for dinner.

Mama says giving you 23 pictures of me was 22 pictures too many. I don't think so. Here is one more for you. AND, here is a zucchini blossom.

I am reading up on new babies and I have some free advice: Do NOT hug that grandbaby too much. It isn't good for her.

I hope they name her Hortense. That's a <u>great</u> name, don't you think?

Woe Is Me,

your (almost only—darn!) granddaughter, Ruby L.

Pee Ess: What did you eat on the plane? Not zucchini, I bet. I guess I will go to the Pink Palace and check on the chickens.

Love, Ruby Lavender

Love,
Ruby Lavender

DEBORAH WILES

Gulliver Books
Harcourt, Inc.

Orlando Austin New York San Diego Toronto London

www.HarcourtBooks.com

First Gulliver Books paperback edition 2002
Gulliver Books is a trademark of Harcourt, Inc., registered in
the United States of America and/or other jurisdictions.

The Library of Congress has cataloged an earlier edition
as follows:
Wiles, Debbie.
Love, Ruby Lavender/Deborah Wiles.
p.   cm.
"Gulliver Books."
Summary: When her quirky grandmother goes to Hawaii for
the summer, nine-year-old Ruby learns to survive on her own
in Mississippi by writing letters, befriending chickens as well
as the new girl in town, and finally coping with her
grandfather's death.
[1. Grandparents—Fiction.   2. Self-reliance—Fiction.
3. Death—Fiction.   4. Chickens—Fiction.   5. Mississippi—
Fiction.]   I. Title.
PZ7.W6474Lo   2001
[Fic]—dc21   00-11159
ISBN 0-15-202314-3
ISBN 0-15-205478-2 pb

Text set in Berling
Designed by Lydia D'moch
Map by Ruby Lavender
Compass holder: Bemmie Lavender

A C E G H F D B

For my mother and father,
Marie Kilgore Edwards and Thomas P. Edwards,
with love and gratitude

Acknowledgments

I owe my Aunt Beth McBrayer a Ruby-sized thanks for valuing oral history and taping family stories, especially the one about her chick Rosebud who, it turned out, was really a rooster named Bud; also to Aunt Mitt, who taught me to smell the earth after it rained; Nanny, who showed me how to love a garden; my grandmother, the real Miss Eula; and my dad, the director of "Miss Eula Goes to Hawaii," a home-movie classic that provided lots of inspiration, as did the town of Louin, Mississippi, a place populated with people who live on in my heart just as they did in my childhood.

While writing this book I spent a lot of time swooning, dabbing my forehead with a lace handkerchief, and generally torturing anyone who would listen to me. Lots of credit goes to the torturees, particularly my family: Hannah (who read the manuscript many times), Zach, Jason, Alisa, and Steven, whom I claim as my own; four lions: Nancy Werlin, Joanne Stanbridge, Dian Curtis Regan, and Jane Kurtz; Pophamites Jackie Briggs Martin, Franny Billingsley, and Toni Buzzeo, steadfast friends Norma Chapman, Tana Fletcher, Sue Fortin, Deborah Hopkinson, Cindy Powell, Kay Sheiss; and my teacher, Nancy Johnson. All supplied, at one time or another, Moon Pies, cold cloths, and smelling salts.

Lots of love, a crepe-paper dress, and a bushel basket full of thanks go to my editor, Liz Van Doren, who is no chicken. She stuck with this story, and with me, for more than four years, challenging me to do better, do better, do better. She encouraged me enough, championed me enough, and frustrated me enough that finally I did. She's a pretty good editor . . . for a Yankee.

Love, Ruby Lavender

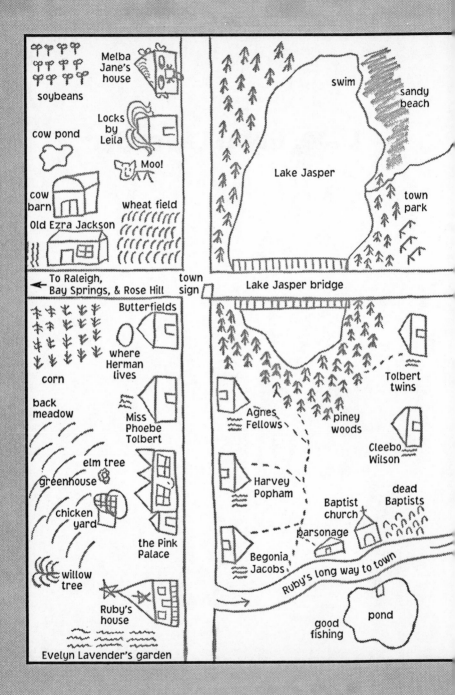

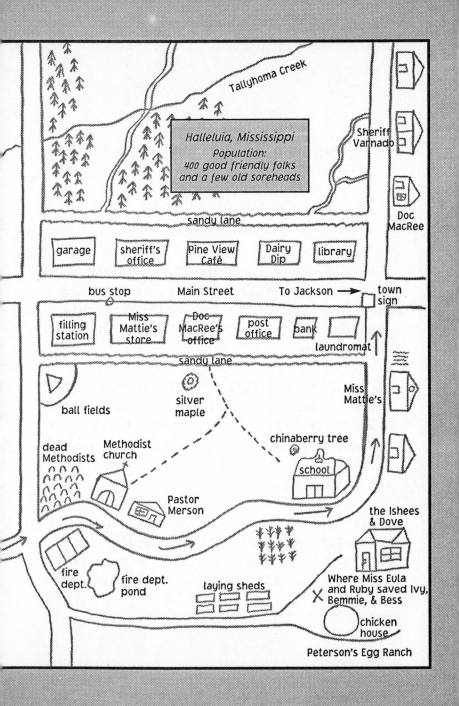

AURORA COUNTY NEWS

Twilight Edition, June 3

Agricultural Page

Halleluia, Mississippi—In a surprise announcement today, Lucius Peterson, of Peterson's Egg Ranch, declared that he would close his shop and retire, after 45 years in the egg business.

"I was planning this," said Peterson. "I haven't bought new chicks for two years now. These old hens are ready to go to slaughter—pretty soon you'll be seeing them on your dinner plates as drumsticks and chicken`a la king."

Local citizen Miss Eula Dapplevine, long known for her commitment to animal rights and lost causes, was heard to say in response, "That's what you think, buster."

June 4

Murderers! You can't have them *all*!" Ruby Lavender leaned out the car window and shook her fist. The car lurched to a halt in the dirt yard of Peterson's Egg Ranch, and Ruby scrambled out the door. She ran in bare feet as fast as she could into a dusty sea of chickens—a sea of chickens being herded toward their death at the chopping block.

Miss Eula Dapplevine was driving the getaway car. She leaped from her seat into the hot June sun and waved her arms wildly. "Run, run! Run for your lives!"

Chickens screeched and panicked. They ran and jumped and flapped their wings.

Ruby opened her arms and swept herself, like a wave, through the squawking.

"Gotcha!" She dropped to her knees and reached for chicken legs and necks and breasts, pulling them to her. "*I'll* save you, girls!" She had a face full of feathers. She swayed from side to side, trying to get her balance. Her left overalls strap slipped off her shoulder.

Three men came running from inside the chicken house. The tallest one jerked down the bandanna he wore around his mouth and nose. "Stop! Thieves! Get back here with those hens!"

"Go away, Lucius!" yelled Miss Eula. She waved dust from her face with her big hat. "You won't miss a few old laying hens past their prime!" Ruby struggled to stand with her arms full of chickens. She staggered to the car, a squawking hen under each arm, and tossed them through the open window of the backseat. "Hit it, Miss Eula!" Another hen ran screaming straight for Ruby and nearly knocked her down. Ruby grabbed it. "Good garden of peas! Well, get in here!"

She tossed it into the car, then climbed through the open window right behind it.

"Hurry, Miss Eula!"

"You're crazy, Eula!" shouted Lucius. "Crazy!"

Chickens flew at Lucius, pecking his hard boots. Others raced, like a river over a dam, through the split-rail fence, across the country road, and into the surrounding fields.

"Go, girls, go!" Miss Eula put her hands on her hips. "How would *you* like to be on someone's dinner plate, Lucius? Lucius à la king!" Lucius and his workers didn't know which way to run first as they tried to shush the puddle of chickens left at their feet.

Miss Eula flounced back into the car. She jerked the gearshift into drive and pulled out of Peterson's Egg Ranch, weaving the big car slowly right and left as she dodged chickens and stirred up dust. "How many did we get?"

"We got three! They're red!" Next to Ruby sat three of the most pitiful-looking, nervous creatures she had ever laid eyes on. They clucked and stared at her.

"Three, that's a good number. A lucky number. *You* are a good partner, Ruby Lavender...for a *nine-year-old*." Miss Eula winked at Ruby.

"And *you* are a good getaway driver...for a *grandmother*." Ruby winked back.

"Folks will keep eating chicken, all right, but they won't eat these three, now, will they?"

"They surely won't," said Ruby. "I can't wait to get to know them."

"We'll get to know them together."

The car traveled smoothly down the country road. The chickens squawked and flapped and put up a ruckus. Miss Eula's and Ruby's eyes met in the rearview mirror. They smiled at each other....They giggled....And then they laughed and laughed.

June 6

Ruby finished the letter she was writing and folded it three times quickly. She jumped up, knocking her chair backward, and shoved the note into the big front pocket of her overalls. Then she raced outside, slapping the screen door against the house.

Her mother sat cross-legged in the vegetable garden next to giant hills of zucchini, scribbling into a notebook in her lap. She looked up, squinting under the brim of her straw hat. "Whoa! What's the emergency?"

"Got mail to deliver!" called Ruby. "Important mail! A matter of life and death!"

"Be home for supper, if you're still alive!"

Ruby waved a hand raggedly and ran. Her bare feet slapped the dirt road, and her ponytailed red hair leaped all over the place, like a fire chasing her down the hill.

She took the long way into town. She always did,

since the accident. When she came to the town sign, she leaned against it to catch her breath.

WELCOME
to Halleluia, Mississippi

Population:
400 Good Friendly Folks
And a Few Old Soreheads

Every storefront in Halleluia faced Main Street. Behind the stores ran a sandy lane. Ruby followed it past the back of the Laundromat and the bank, to the post office. She patted her pocket. Yes, the note was still there.

Behind the post office grew a majestic silver maple tree. Its roots stretched themselves out underground, popping up here and there, knobby, like big scraped knees. Hidden in a root tangle was a dry hole just big enough for a sack of marbles or a softball. But Ruby never put her softball into this hole—it was her secret mailbox. She pulled the letter from her pocket, to put it in the knothole.

But wait! She had mail! It was pink. First she made sure no one was looking. The Tolbert twins were farther up the lane, jumping rope—they didn't notice her. Old Ezra Jackson dozed in a chair behind the filling station. Ruby yanked the paper from the knothole and replaced it with her letter. She sat under the silver maple with the piece of pink paper and read.

June 6

Dear Ruby,
     Today will be a busy day in the store. I can't wait to see you, even though we won't have time to drink a Yoo-Hoo together, like we usually do. I will be anxious for a report on Ivy, Bemmie, and Bess.
               Love,
               your favorite (only) grandmother,
               Miss Eula

Ruby had a report, all right. She couldn't wait to tell Miss Eula what had happened. It was all in the letter she had just put in the knothole. She would let Miss Eula know it was waiting for her.

She walked past the back of the post office, past the back of Doc MacRee's office. Yes sir, she had news! She felt puffed up and full of importance. She sauntered, pleased as she could be, through the back door of Miss Mattie Perkins's general store.

June 6

Dear Miss Eula,

Oh joy and happy day! Ivy has laid three eggs! I can't believe it! Bemmie is so jealous! She is clucking all over the place. Ivy is saved from the chopping block, AND she is going to have chicks of her own!

What time will you be done working today, so we can visit the chickens together? The eggs are brown.

Love,

your favorite (only) grandchild,

Ruby L.

2

Miss Mattie Perkins's mercantile was stuffed with everything anybody ever could want or need. Coffee beans and crackers were piled in big barrels. Overalls, work boots, and gloves were stacked on low wooden tables. A tall cooler stuffed full of homemade butter, fresh eggs, and Grapette pop hummed a low buzz all day.

Miss Mattie spotted Ruby coming through the door. "Just in time! Come over here, child, and help me with this box." Miss Mattie was wrestling with a ladder and trying to reach a shoe box on the top shelf of the back room.

Ruby glanced around for any sign of Miss Eula but didn't see her. She gave Miss Mattie a wan smile. "Would you like me to get those shoes for you, Miss Mattie?"

"You could be of some use, if you did."

Ruby scrambled up the ladder and grabbed the box.

Miss Mattie brushed at the front of her dress. "I sent Eula to check the mail." She patted her frizzled hair into place. Ruby handed her the shoe box and stepped down the ladder rungs to the floor.

As Miss Mattie took the box, the sound of children laughing and the *ping-ping-ping!* of something spilling across the wooden floor stopped her short. "What's that?" She grabbed a broom. "For pity's sake! It's those Latham children in the coffee beans. And here we've got more customers than you can shake a stick at. I *told* Eula to hurry." She shoved the box at Ruby. "Here, come help me with these shoes— they're for Leila Latham. She's been waiting for ten minutes already and those children won't let her think. You help her out—it will give you something to do while you wait."

Ruby's heart jumped into her throat. She fumbled the box, then dropped it. "But Miss Mattie... I can't..." Ruby tried to get her aunt's attention, but Miss Mattie was already halfway across the store, waving her broom and shouting commands. Ruby's shoulders fell. She picked up the box, took a deep breath, and walked out of the back room and into the rich, warm smells of the general store. She felt herself deflating with every step, but still she held on to her important news and hoped Miss Eula might check the knothole for mail, too.

Leila Latham didn't seem to notice the commotion around the coffee barrel. She was deep in conversation with Mr. Harvey Popham. Ruby approached her slowly, hoping with every breath that the woman would stand up and decide to leave the mercantile. But she didn't. Worse, as Ruby got closer, Mrs. Latham's eldest daughter, Melba Jane, flounced into the seat next to her mother and smiled at Ruby—a quick sugar-sweet smile that vanished as soon as her skirts settled.

Melba wore seven satin ribbons in her smooth brown hair and a million thumbtacks on the bottom of her hard-soled shoes. Now she *tap-tap-tapp*ed the floor from her seat and glowered at Ruby. Ruby's fingers turned cold around the shoe box and she swallowed hard.

Mrs. Latham's voice was soft. "How are you, Ruby?"

"Fine," Ruby said. Mrs. Latham smiled, and Ruby relaxed her grip on the shoe box. "Here's your shoes." She tried a smile back, as she stuck the box out in front of her. Melba Jane kept *tap-tap-tap*ping the floor and staring at Ruby.

"Help me try these on, will you?" Melba's mother went back to her conversation with Mr. Harvey as if nothing unusual had happened, as if she'd talked to Ruby every day since last summer's accident. Ruby began lacing the new shoes. She felt Melba's eyes on her and listened to her *tap-tap-tap*, louder and faster, until she could stand it no longer.

"What's the *matter* with you, Melba Jane?"

Melba let a slow grin spread across her face. She slid down in her seat so the heels of her shoes touched the floor, *ta-tap-ta-tippety-tap.*

"*Cluck!*" she whispered. "*Cluck-cluck-cluck!*"

Ruby's face grew hot. "Stop it, Melba Jane."

Melba Jane slid all the way out of her chair, *tap-tap-thunk,* and squatted on the floor, her hands in her armpits, her elbows out and waving like a chicken's wings.

"Stop that!"

Melba shot Ruby a loony, bug-eyed look. "*Bwauck! Bwauck-bwauck-bwauck!*"

"Shut up!" Ruby jumped to her feet. "You just shut up!"

Mrs. Latham was startled out of her conversation with Mr. Harvey. "What's the matter?"

Miss Mattie had corralled the younger Latham children and was trying mightily to shove them out the front door. Now she jerked her attention toward Ruby and Melba Jane.

Melba's eyebrows shot up, her lips formed a crooked O of pretend fright, and she shrank from Ruby with little *tippy-taps*. She flapped her elbows and swooned. Then she stopped, stuck out her chin, and spit a word at Ruby. "Chicken!"

Ruby bared her teeth, flung her arms over her head, and made her hands into claws. Then she lunged for Melba Jane. *"Aaarrrrggghhh!"*

A look of genuine panic mixed with surprise flew across Melba's face. It only took her a second to scream, *"Mamaaa!" Tap-tap-tap-tap-tap-tap-tap!* She flew toward the front door of the mercantile, slamming into Miss Mattie as she ran. Miss Mattie spun around like a whirligig as Melba Jane scrambled through the pile of little Lathams at the doorway, flattening most of them. Ruby was right behind Melba, her claw hands reaching for her. Little Lathams squealed. Miss Mattie clutched the coatrack for dear life.

Ruby reached the door and prepared to hurtle over the little Lathams. Instead, she hurtled into Miss Eula, walking through the door with a pile of mail.

3

Ummmph!" Miss Eula clutched Ruby to her, and together they fell into the pile of Lathams. Mail and Lathams spluttered across the porch planks. Melba Jane ran down the sidewalk, still screaming. Little Lathams began picking themselves up and gathering mail.

"Eula?" Miss Mattie gave her hair a weak pat.

"You all right, Mattie? Ruby?"

"Yes, ma'am."

The smaller children were dazed but finally quiet. One of them handed Miss Eula the mail. "Thank you, darlin'." She waved it at Miss Mattie. "No shirt buttons today, but there's a crate of garden tools, waiting for somebody strong to carry it over. What's happening here?"

"I don't know yet—but I intend to find out." Miss

Mattie straightened her dress and pulled herself together. Customers crowded the front door to see what had happened. "For heaven's sake! It's not a sideshow!" Folks drifted back inside, and the everyday noise of the store picked up. Mrs. Latham had gathered her children, whispered something to Miss Mattie, and was out the door, following Melba's screams.

Ruby edged toward the sidewalk.

"You come back here, young lady!" Miss Mattie's eyes were full of fire.

"Now, Mattie." Miss Eula brushed herself off. "No harm done. You know as well as I do, those Latham children have become uncontrollable!"

Miss Mattie shook her finger at Ruby, then fished a handkerchief out of her apron pocket and mopped her forehead. "I know Leila has her hands full these days with Lionel gone. I hate that she does. But someone needs to speak to her about those children."

"Maybe someone will. But it's probably best if it doesn't come from us."

Miss Mattie stuffed her handkerchief back into her apron pocket and eyeballed Miss Eula. "I need help." She went inside, and the screen door slapped behind her.

Miss Eula sat down beside Ruby on the top step

of the porch. Ruby turned toward her and spread her arms out wide. "She made fun of me and the chickens! She squawked like a chicken! She *called* me a chicken!" Ruby stared intently into Miss Eula's face.

Miss Eula stared straight ahead, looking at nothing. "It's so hot you can hear the dust blow."

"What am I going to do about Melba?" Ruby blew strings of red hair out of her face.

Miss Eula gave Ruby a sympathetic look. "I don't know, sugar; I wish I knew. She wants you to feel as bad as she does, that's all. Can you ignore her? Make her float away in your mind…"

"You should have heard her! *'Bwauck-bwauck-bwauck!'*—right in front of me and the whole store!"

A honeysuckle vine curled around the porch railing. Miss Eula picked a blossom and handed it to Ruby. Ruby pulled the stem through to get a drop of nectar on her tongue. Miss Eula twisted off some thin branches of honeysuckle and began weaving them in a circle, like a wreath—leaves, buds, and all.

"You know, Ruby, Melba acts brave but she's scared underneath. Just look at how she skedaddled out of here. Imagine what it must be like for her and her family, since her daddy died. There are so many children in that house, and she's the oldest—imagine being the oldest of six when you are only nine!—and her mama depends on her now more than ever." She plunked the honeysuckle wreath on Ruby's head. "Poor old Melba."

"Poor old Melba!" Ruby shot up from the steps. The wreath skimmed off her head but she caught it. "Poor old *me*!"

A letter dropped from Miss Eula's lap to the step. She scooped it up and changed the subject. "Ruby! I almost forgot. I've got wonderful mail here, from your uncle Johnson and aunt Annette." She waved an airmail envelope in front of Ruby. The postmark read HONOLULU.

Ruby didn't notice. "Good garden of peas, Miss Eula! I forgot *my* big news. You'll never believe it." She jammed the wreath onto her head so it wouldn't fall off. It made her whole head smell sweet.

Miss Eula smiled and tucked Johnson's letter into her apron pocket. "I just might, sugar, since I've already read your mail."

"You got it! Good, I was hoping you'd picked up *all* your mail."

"I got it and I left you some, as well."

"Isn't it a miracle about Ivy! She's going to be a mother!"

"It's a wonderful surprise, Ruby! Let me get to

the end of this busy day, and we can visit the chickens together. What do you say?"

"Yes, yes, yes!" Ruby's heart lifted. "I'll go check my mail right now."

Miss Eula reached into her apron pocket. "Here's a lemon drop for helping Miss Mattie. She appreciates your help, sugar."

"No, she doesn't." Ruby plopped the lemon drop in her mouth and tried to talk around it. It clacked on her teeth. "Miss Mattie is a crab."

"Well, she's got a lot on her mind, honey. When your grandpa died, she lost her brother…Now she has all the responsibility for the store on her shoulders."

Ruby choked as she tried to change the subject. Miss Eula pumped her once on the back, and Ruby coughed the lemon drop into her hand, then tossed it back into her mouth and wiped her sticky hand on her overalls. Her cheeks puckered with the sour taste, and she talked with a fish mouth. "I've never seen Miss Mattie smile."

Miss Eula chuckled. "Oh, she smiles. But she is who she is, sugar. So is Melba Jane. Aren't we all? Go on, now. I know your mama must have supper waiting."

Ruby hitched up her left overalls strap and stepped into a buttery late-afternoon sun. Long shadows slid across the storefronts, and the air was spangled with dust. The sweet taste of the lemon drop began to come through the sour.

Grandpa Garnet had been the one who had loved lemon drops. He told Ruby most people were like lemon drops, sour and sweet together. She couldn't see it. Grandpa Garnet would have loved the story of saving Ivy, Bemmie, and Bess. And now there were eggs! There was good news. It was so good to share it. And there was no better friend to share it with than Miss Eula.

June 6

Dear Ruby,

What exciting news about Ivy! I'm glad we decided to give the chickens the old greenhouse for a henhouse. It makes a nice home for new chicks, with all those windows!

Let's meet at the Pink Palace at six o'clock—a lucky hour. I am going to parch some peanuts in the oven.

But FIRST, we will cluck over Ivy. What a gal! So are you.

I have BIG NEWS for you, too. It's a surprise! I will tell you tonight.

> Love,
> your (almost done for the day) grandmother,
> Miss Eula

4

Ruby tucked the pink note in her overalls pocket and ran for home. As she banged through the back door, she smelled the summer's first stewed tomatoes bubbling on the stove. A pile of zucchini spilled across the countertop, along with her mother's notes from the garden. At the top of page one, she had written neatly "Adventures in Zucchini." Ruby washed her face and hands and came to the table, damp.

"It's you!" said Ruby's mother. "Glad to see you're still alive. Nice hat." She put a basket of hot biscuits on the table and sat down. "I almost went looking for you."

Ruby flopped herself into a chair. "I came home the long way." She put her wreath hat in the middle of the table as a centerpiece.

"The long way again. No wonder you're so out of breath. What was the life-or-death situation?"

Ruby leaned across the table, gloating. "Ivy has laid three eggs!"

"You don't say!"

"I do say!" She helped herself to the biscuits, then the creamed corn and fried okra and a slice of sweet-potato pie. "We thought these hens were way too old for laying, but it turns out Ivy had other plans. I can't wait to meet her chicks."

"You don't think there will be chicks!" Ruby's mother poured sweet iced tea into two tall glasses.

"Sure there will be chicks. Don't you remember Herman, the Butterfields' rooster? For the past two days, we've been shooing him out of the chicken yard until the Butterfields fixed their gate and we *got* a gate. Now ole Herman's going to be a daddy."

Ruby buttered biscuits: two for her mother, three for her. Her mother put her elbows on the table and rested her chin in her hands. "Life does go on."

"That's what I heard you tell Miss Eula after church last week."

"That's what she taught me. I was just reminding her. This year has been hard for her."

Ruby's heart skipped a beat, and she spoke quickly. "But it's been a whole year." She shoved a

biscuit at her mother. "Miss Eula is fine now. Just
fine." Ruby took a big bite of biscuit.

"Some losses leave great big holes, Ruby. It's hard
to lose someone you love so deeply, especially when
you've known them as long as Miss Eula knew your
grandpa."

Ruby talked with her mouth full and changed
the subject. "I had a hard time today, too." Crumbs
sprinkled her overalls and butter slid down her chin.

"Do tell."

Ruby held up a freckled finger and finished
chewing, then swallowed. "At Miss Mattie's store,
Melba Jane started picking on me, making fun, acting
like a chicken…then she *called* me a chicken…"

"Goodness! Then what happened?"

Ruby took a sloshy gulp of iced tea and wiped
her whole face with her napkin. "I lit out after her."

"Ruby!"

"But I didn't tackle her; she got away."

Ruby's mother opened her mouth to say something, then shut it. Instead, she reached over and cap-
tured Ruby's chin gently in the cupped palm of her
hand. "What *am* I going to do with you?"

Ruby tried a grin. "You're going to love me."

"That I do." Her mother sat back and picked up

her iced tea. She swirled it around to cool it, and the ice cubes tinkled against the glass. The mantel clock kept time in the living room, a solid *tock-tock, tock-tock*, and for a moment time stretched out and away. Ruby thought about how she and her grandpa used to wind the clock together, every week, and the words came out before she could stop them. "I miss Grandpa Garnet."

"Me, too, sweetie. I expect I'm always going to miss my daddy. He loved us to pieces, didn't he?"

Ruby gave herself over to memory. "He always let me have the first scoop of ice cream when we made it ourselves."

"He taught me to whistle, and how to play poker."

"Miss Eula says she played strip poker with Grandpa Garnet."

"Ruby!"

"Well, she did…"

Ruby's mother laughed. "I'm *quite* sure she did…"

Ruby sighed. "He would have loved Ivy, Bemmie, and Bess."

"I expect he would have. It's good to see his greenhouse being used this summer."

"Good garden of peas! I forgot—I've got to go!"

Ruby almost fell out of her chair. "Miss Eula and I are going to visit the chickens tonight and see Ivy's eggs. And Miss Eula has big news for me!"

Ruby's mother stood up. "Well, take her a plate. She loves my sweet-potato pie…and goodness knows she won't cook for herself." She followed Ruby to the sink, where she kissed the top of her daughter's head. "Be back before the crow calls. And no more raids on any egg ranches."

The Pink Palace glowed in the early evening sunset. Big old hydrangeas—snowball bushes, Ruby called them—bloomed the length of the front porch. Grandpa Garnet had planted them before Ruby was born. He was the gardener in the family. "That's where your mama gets her green thumb," Miss Eula had told Ruby. "It's no wonder she's so smart about flowers and vegetables and bugs and such. She was digging in the dirt in the dark before she could talk!"

Ruby remembered doing the same thing with her grandfather. He had told her that corn was the tallest when you planted it under a new moon. He taught her to soak her moonflower seeds before she planted them. Every year they planted zinnias and marigolds and bachelor buttons and geraniums together, but no one had planted them this year. Still, there were flowers that returned year after year, and here they were, blooming their heads off in the front yard, the side, the back, all over—flower beds full of hollyhocks and bee balm and lemon verbena and peppermint and black-eyed Susans, her grandpa's favorite. Ruby picked one now and stuck the flower stem behind her ear. The golden petals tickled her face.

Ruby and Miss Eula had painted the house "Shell-shocked Pink" late last summer, after Grandpa Garnet died. Miss Eula had said it was a rite of passage.

Rite of passage. It made Ruby think about traveling through secret tunnels and passageways and having her ticket punched at different checkpoints. She had the feeling, painting the house, that they were doing just that. One day they had splattered themselves silly, laughing and crying and telling stories about themselves and Grandpa Garnet. If he had been there, he would have directed the painting. "A little more here! You missed a spot there!" He would have made tomato sandwiches for them at lunch. He would have taken pictures.

But he wasn't there, so they did it themselves with no audience but the nosy neighbors, who drove by the house slowwwly or peeked out from behind their venetian blinds. Miss Eula had waved a messy paintbrush at all of them.

Ruby blinked herself out of her memories. She stood and hiked up her left overalls strap. She and Miss Eula had a ritual they followed each evening. Ruby faced the Pink Palace, put her hands on her hips, leaned her head backward into the early summer evening, and called, "Oh, Miss Euuuuuuulaaaaa! Can you come out and play?"

And Miss Eula did.

5

Let's get this straight." Ruby leaned over Miss Eula's kitchen table, an old issue of *Poultry Today* spread in front of her. "Twenty-one days from egg to chick. That means we should have some babies before July!"

"Let's see. Laid today, means chicks on..." Miss Eula counted on her fingers, "June twenty-seventh. Or maybe twenty-sixth, depending on what time these eggs were laid. Either way, that's a lucky day."

The kitchen smelled like peanut butter and the table was littered with peanut shells. Two empty bottles of Orange Crush and a Mason jar full of black-eyed Susans sat among the shells. The attic fan droned and shoved the hot air around the room. Miss Eula wore one of the muumuus her son, Johnson, had sent her over the years. It had purple flowers on it.

Ruby sat back in her chair and smiled. "Ivy looks as shiny as a new penny."

"Yes, indeed," agreed Miss Eula. "And don't you love how jealous Bemmie is! All full of clucks and squawks and 'Let me see, let me see!'"

"Now can you tell me your big surprise? The one you told me about in your note?"

"I can. Ruby, let's take a walk to the back meadow. That's a good place for my surprise. I'll bring the quilt and the softball; you bring the gloves. There's still enough light to have a catch."

"Yes, ma'am!" Ruby grabbed the floppy hats by the back door, plopped one on her head, and gave the other to Miss Eula. "I love big news. I can't wait to hear about what we're going to do next."

The back meadow shimmered with sound. Ruby and Miss Eula walked through the flowering meadow grass, holding hands in the last wash of daylight, listening to the *zizz, zizz, zizz* of life around them. The moon was beginning to rise, a crescent moon, the color of old teeth.

"Here we are," said Miss Eula. "So nice of this willow tree to keep our spot for us."

They spread out their quilt under the willow in the warm purple light.

"I do love this quilt," said Miss Eula. "It holds good memories, doesn't it?"

Ruby straightened a corner. "Yes, ma'am, it does." The quilt was sewn in a pattern of stars made from pieces of old clothing: Ruby's old overalls, her baby blanket, her red shorts, her button blouses. Miss Eula's wild aprons were in there, as well as two everyday dresses and some striped dish towels. Grandpa Garnet had donated his favorite flannel shirt for the corner stars. Between the stars was a path of pink, made from an old set of sheets. Ruby and Miss Eula had sewn every stitch themselves. It was a masterpiece.

Ruby put the ball and gloves by the tree trunk. She sighed and let go of the hard day as she flopped herself onto the quilt. A breeze began a little *puff-puff* around them as Miss Eula slipped off her shoes and sat beside Ruby. Her muumuu spread out around her, making her look like the center of a giant flower. A firefly winked on, and Miss Eula reached out her knobby hand to catch it.

"Look, Miss Ruby, what I've got."

The first firefly! Miss Eula gave it to Ruby, and she held it between her cupped palms. "*Oh, Little One, Bright One.*" She recited the rhyme her grandfather had taught her:

"You are the first one, so you are the light.
You are the one we follow tonight.
Fly away now to your free life—so sweet!
We'll follow you with our true hearts till we meet
on the side of the shore, in the meadow so fair,
in the place where our souls soar into the air…"

Ruby parted her palms and lifted them upward. The firefly winked once and flew into the darkening sky, winked again, and was gone.

"I believe that *is* the first firefly tonight." Miss Eula's voice was sifty and far away.

"What's the matter, Miss Eula?"

"Oh, sugar, I've been thinking tonight about you, me, your grandpa, your mama…about Johnson and Annette…oh, about life and how it does go on."

"Mama says you taught her that. I heard her say it to you, too, last Sunday after church."

"Well, your mama needed to hear that a long time ago, when she found out she'd be raising you all by herself. And she did go on; we all did. Now it's my time to go on. And I will."

"What does that mean? Are you going somewhere?" Ruby felt a tingle across her shoulders.

"I am, sugar." Miss Eula's voice caught in her throat. "I am."

Ruby blinked. "Where? Where are you going?"

"I'm taking a trip, Ruby honey. I'm going to go visit Johnson and Annette in Hawaii."

"Hawaii!" Ruby held her breath. "When? Why?"

"The day after tomorrow." Miss Eula's voice picked up its old sturdiness. "Remember the letter I waved at you at Miss Mattie's store? There's good news in Hawaii, Ruby. Johnson and Annette had a baby! They kept it a secret, and now they are telling everyone. And I'm invited to come to Hawaii and be with them. I'm going to take me a trip. They sent a ticket with the letter."

Ruby felt the earth open up to swallow her. "Wait!" She scrambled to her feet.

"Ruby, it's all right, listen to me—"

"No! You can't be leaving!"

"I'm not leaving forever, Ruby."

Ruby felt light-headed. "When does the ticket say you come back?"

"It's a round-trip ticket to Hawaii, with an open return. That means I can pick the date I come back."

"It means you don't have to come back at all!" Ruby turned her back to Miss Eula and kicked her catcher's mitt. The inside of her nose got that stinging feeling it got whenever she was about to cry. "I don't want you to leave! You can't! If you leave, you leave me alone with Miss Mattie and that awful Melba Jane!" Ruby held back her tears, but her shoulders shook.

Miss Eula got to her feet and tried to put her arms around Ruby, but Ruby took two steps away. A willow branch brushed her face, and she shoved it aside.

"Please don't go. I need you to stay here with me."

"I'm leaving because I need to, Ruby. I need to do what's right for me. *And* for you. I want to see how life does go on, and then I want to come back to you and your mama and my home."

Ruby sniffed back tears and wiped at her eyes. "You'll get over there and forget all about this place. You won't remember me! You've got a new grand-baby now—I can't believe you haven't told Mama about this yet."

"I wanted to tell you first, sugar. I just read John-son's letter this afternoon, and the news was as much a surprise to me as it is to you. I had no idea—"

"How can Uncle Johnson send you a ticket *now*, when *he* couldn't come home last summer, for... well, you know..." Ruby stopped.

"Johnson just sold his first paintings, Ruby, so he has enough extra money to either fly here by himself, or let me fly there to see him and Annette and the new baby. You know, it pained him no end that he couldn't get here for Garnet's funeral last summer. Pained me, too."

Ruby sank down, down, into her quilt. "What's this new grandbaby's name?"

"She doesn't have one yet. But her name won't be Ruby, and she won't be you, and she will never, never take your place."

"You'll love her anyway."

Miss Eula laughed and sat down next to Ruby. "Of course I will! I do! But I love you, too, and what's more, I'm depending on you. Who else is going to look after Ivy, Bemmie, and Bess for me? Who's going to take care of the new chicks? Who's going to gather my mail and keep the Pink Palace in shape? No one can do it like you can."

"I *can't* do all that by myself."

"Sure you can. You'll have your mama here to help you, and you have your friends—"

"Mama's busy—this is her busy season!—and everybody I like lives too far out of town."

"—and you'll write to me and tell me how Ivy is doing, and I'll write to you and tell you how Hawaii is, and we'll just keep right on doing what we've always done."

"Who's going to keep me from tackling Melba Jane and scratching her eyes out?"

Miss Eula smiled. "You'll do a fine job of that all by yourself."

"You always know what to say about her to make me feel better."

"I'll keep saying it, Ruby honey. And you'll keep remembering it. It will be fine."

Ruby lay on her side and curled her body into a ball. She buried her face in the sweet smell of her quilt. "When will you be back?"

"I'll be back when I've had time to soak up Johnson and Annette and the baby. When I've talked and talked about your grandpa. When I've lived away from reminders of Garnet for a while. When I've made some new memories."

"When you've lived away from me for a while."

Ruby unrolled herself and looked through the branches of the willow. The moon's light sprinkled over Miss Eula and Ruby, sparkling them like diamonds. It was going to be a beautiful night. Miss Eula lay next to Ruby. She took Ruby's hand and they lay on their quilt, next to each other, breathing together, being together.

"I'm taking you with me, Ruby girl. I'm taking you in my dreams. And you'll come to me in your letters. You *will* write me, won't you? I think you're a pretty good writer…for a *nine-year-old*."

Ruby's voice was full of cracks. "And you're a pretty good scribbler yourself…for a *grandmother*."

Miss Eula squeezed Ruby's hand. "Oh, Miss Ruby Lavender, you do pull at my heart. Look up at this starry sky. We are like those shining stars, Ruby. We will be under this same sky, no matter where we are. You remember that."

Ruby squeezed back. Warm tears slipped sideways down her cheeks and into her ears. She held Miss Eula's hand and thought about the lonely, empty summer ahead.

6

June 8

"For pity's sake!" Miss Mattie was exasperated. "You'd think we were selling tickets to see snow in July!"

Miss Mattie's store was also the Greyhound bus depot in Halleluia. Each morning at 6:45, the bus stopped in front of the store on the way to Jackson. It came back through the opposite direction every evening at 8:00. Most days the town was still shut up tight when the bus rolled in, but not today. Miss Mattie had opened the store, "Just to keep people from spilling into the highway and getting run over flat."

Ruby was behind the nail kegs inside Miss Mattie's store, sitting on a paint bucket. It was a good spot from which to hear and see all the action. She peered between the eight-penny and six-penny nails. There was Melba Jane with her mother and her five brothers and sisters. They swarmed around the Greyhound sign that hung from the light pole out front. The little ones were tugging and hitting each other, arguing about something. Melba Jane left them and scooted inside Miss Mattie's store, *ta-tap-ta-tappety-tap*, giggling with Lorna Mullins, another tappety girl and a sixth grader. Ruby watched Lorna take two pretzels from the cracker barrel and give one to Melba Jane. Melba removed a glove and took it, with a conspiratorial smile.

Phoebe "Scoop" Tolbert stood outside with Miss Mattie. Miss Phoebe always smelled like violets—powdered up one side and down the other with talcum. She wrote a column for the *Aurora County News* called "Happenings in Halleluia."

Miss Mattie sounded peeved. "I don't know why you want to report it in the paper, Phoebe. The whole town is here to witness it."

Miss Phoebe lifted her head and sniffed. "We owe it to our elderly readers, those who cannot be with us today."

Miss Mattie harrumphed. "The only bodies who are not here today are in the cemetery!"

Miss Eula drove her big car slowly up Main Street. "Mattie!" She waved out the window and pulled the car into the space reserved for the bus.

Ruby's mother leaned across Miss Eula and called to Miss Mattie. "Have you seen Ruby? We can't find her anywhere!"

"Not yet. Move the car, Eula! Unless you want it run over."

Ruby's mother opened the trunk and took out her mother's bags. "Come on, Mama. I know Ruby is here somewhere. I'll park this thing for you. You come say good-bye to your public."

Miss Eula eased out of the car and looped her big white purse over her arm. She wore a beige dress with buttons up the front, a belt at the waist, stockings and white shoes, and a round beige hat. And gloves! Lipstick! Ruby stared at her. "You'd think she was going to church!"

Folks crowded Miss Eula, full of good-trip messages, come-back messages, give-Johnson-our-best, squeeze-that-baby-for-us, send-us-a-picture-postcard messages.

"Bus!" yelled two small boys standing in the road. Their mothers ran to catch them and bring them back to the sidewalk. Ruby's mother appeared, back from parking the car. "I don't see her."

Miss Eula peered over heads. "She told me she would never say good-bye. I guess she meant it."

The big Greyhound slowed and coughed and wheezed onto the shoulder of Main Street in front of Miss Mattie's store, spewing a trail of black exhaust. The driver opened the door and looked puzzled. "What have we here, a convention? How many of you folks for Jackson?"

Miss Eula stepped forward. "Just me."

"She's going to the airport!" said a small voice, one of the boys who had been in the road. "She's riding on an airplane! She's going to Hawaii!"

The driver smiled wide. "My stars! Then it's a party!" He shoved his hat back on his head and opened the doors on the underside of the Greyhound. He picked up Miss Eula's bags and began storing them in the belly of the bus. The early morning sunshine was sharp and clean and sparkled on the bus windows.

Miss Eula turned. "I know you all will miss me!" Laughter rolled around the crowd. "I will miss you, that's for certain. Mostly I will miss your many kindnesses to me this past year." People fell silent.

"Harvey Popham, everyone should have a neighbor as thoughtful as you are. I thank you for your advice and your butter beans. Agnes Fellows, I thank you for your pop-in visits, and for riding with me to the Eastern Star meetings. Begonia Jacobs, I have you to thank for keeping me informed about what everybody *else* thought I should be doing this last year!"

Mrs. Jacobs threw her hands out at Miss Eula and laughed.

Miss Eula spotted Melba's mother. "Leila." The crowd hushed. "Take care of yourself. I will miss you." Miss Eula blew her a kiss. Melba's mother caught it in her hand, placed it on her cheek, and smiled. Melba wheeled and walked stiffly up the street, where she sat on the curb and pulled her dress over her knees.

Miss Mattie cleared her throat.

"Mattie!" Miss Eula's voice was warm and full of love. "I know I leave you shorthanded in the store, but I have no doubt you will decide how to handle that."

"You're going to go whether I say so or not, so go. Tell my nephew hello. And remember you're a grandmother—don't go climbing any coconut trees."

The bus driver took off his hat and looked apologetic. "We got to get going, ma'am. Got a schedule to keep."

Ruby's mother gave Miss Eula a last hug. "Be well. I love you." Miss Eula squeezed her back, then touched Miss Mattie's arm. "I know you love me, too!" Miss Mattie harrumphed and barked to the bus driver, "She's ready! Go! Go!"

Ruby watched Miss Eula board the bus. She thought about running to her for one last hug—a hug that smelled like shimmering meadows and parched peanuts and chicken feathers and pink paint and old-est memories. But she didn't. She stayed right where she was. She would not say good-bye.

People waved from the sidewalk. "Good-bye! Good-bye!"

The engine thrummed like an airplane and the bus pulled slowly onto Main Street. Ruby stood up to get a last look at Miss Eula sitting by the bus window, waving. She saw Melba Jane's mother sit on the curb next to Melba and put her arm around her shoulders and lean toward her daughter. Their heads touched gently.

"Ruby Lavender!" Miss Mattie stood in the door of the mercantile. "Hiding! You were hiding out in my store!"

"Well, yes, ma'am, I mean, no, ma'am, I wasn't hiding exactly..."

"Well, what *were* you doing?"

"I was...I was not saying good-bye."

Miss Mattie gave Ruby a long look. "Child, come here." Ruby climbed over the nail barrels and stood in front of Miss Mattie. Miss Mattie bent over to look Ruby in the eye. She put her face directly in front of Ruby's, and Ruby could see every wrinkle on it. It reminded her of her catcher's glove, all worn and creased. "You know, I didn't get the chance to say good-bye to your grandfather before he died, and I've always regretted it. He was my brother, after all. You should say good-bye whenever you can. You just never know."

"She's not going to die, Miss Mattie! She said she's coming back!"

"Of course she's coming back, child. I didn't mean she wouldn't." Miss Mattie studied Ruby for a moment. "Just look at this ponytail. Turn around. I'll fix it for you."

"I like it this way, Miss Mattie." Ruby's red hair pinwheeled out in seven different directions; it was tangled.

Miss Mattie harrumphed. "Go home and find your mother, then; she's worried about you."

"Yes, ma'am." Ruby scrambled out the back door of the mercantile and into the sun. It was going to be another sticky-hot day. Ruby never wanted to be in the mercantile again without Miss Eula. What would it be like to walk home and pass an empty mailbox? An empty Pink Palace? Maybe she could sit in Miss Eula's house and wait there, alone, until she returned.

AURORA COUNTY NEWS

Twilight Edition, June 8

Happenings in Halleluia

by Phoebe "Scoop" Tolbert
Pastor Leroy Merson visited the Halleluia sick and shut-ins this past Wednesday. On Thursday he enjoyed a dinner of roast beef and potatoes at the home of Miss Phoebe Tolbert.

According to Mrs. Evelyn Lavender, county extension agent for home and garden affairs, peppers should be ready for picking next week.

After a spirited discussion at the town council meeting, during which several members threatened to resign (as usual), the title of this year's Town Operetta will be "How Dear to My Heart Are the Scenes of My Childhood."

Local citizen Miss Eula Dapplevine has departed our fair town for an extended trip to Hawaii, to see her son, Johnson, and his wife and new baby.

According to Miss Mattie Perkins, "My life will be more hectic in the store without her help, but on the other hand, this town could use a breather."

Miss Ruby Lavender was standing with Miss Mattie and was heard to say, "Woe is me."

June 8

Dear Miss Eula,

Well, you are gone. I hope you are happy. I am not.

For your information, Melba Jane is still here. I am working on a disappearing potion to make her vanish.

Mama is in the kitchen, cooking, cooking, cooking. She is still writing about zucchini, so I know what <u>we</u> are having for dinner.

Mama says giving you 23 pictures of me was 22 pictures too many. I don't think so. Here is one more for you. AND, here is a zucchini blossom.

I am reading up on new babies and I have some free advice: Do NOT hug that grandbaby too much. It isn't good for her.

I hope they name her Hortense. That's a <u>great</u> name, don't you think?

Woe Is Me,

your (almost only—darn!) granddaughter,

Ruby L.

Pee Ess: What did you eat on the plane? Not zucchini, I bet. I guess I will go to the Pink Palace and check on the chickens.

Dear Miss Eula,

Time for lunch. You are still gone. I am lonely.

For your information, we are having peanut butter and zucchini sandwiches. Sticky and crunchy at the same time. A taste treat, says Mama. I am not so sure.

My disappearing potion didn't work. I'll think of something else.

Here is another picture for you to remember me by.

More free advice: Always jiggle babies after they eat.

WOE from,
your (most important) grandchild,
Ruby L.

Pee Ess: Ivy, Bemmie, and Bess were dust-bathing all morning. I changed their water and fed them more corn. They are so noisy! Mama says try reading to them. She says reading is calming.

June 9

Dear Miss Eula,

Mama says I am going to use up a tree writing to you if I keep this up. If you come home now, it will save a tree.

For your information, I read the chickens some "A" words in my dictionary. (Not the definitions.) It took me most of the afternoon. They asked me to spend the night, but I came on home. I tucked them in first.

Ivy loves sitting on her eggs. I was worried about her being so high up in that old bushel basket full of straw, but she likes it there. Whenever Ivy gets off her nest to eat, Bemmie jumps on. Then Ivy starts squawking. Bess ignores everything and just eats. It's loud. I had to shout while I read from "accordion" to "adventure."

What is your opinion on itching powder for Melba Jane?

More free advice: It is never too late to change your mind.

> Woe and Love,
> your (wasting away) granddaughter,
> Ruby L.

Pee Ess: I am not wasting away for real, but you never know.

7

June 14

I refuse to go! You can't make me!"

Ruby stomped her bare foot. Her mother sat at the kitchen table, typing her column for the weekly "Home and Garden Report" for the *Aurora County News*. The table was littered with zucchini everything. Zucchini-corn-and-cheese pudding. Cream of zucchini soup. Zucchini boats with mushrooms. Zucchini pancakes. The whole room smelled warm and dark green.

Ruby waved her arms in front of her mother. "Good garden of peas, Mama! I can't go see Miss Mattie without Miss Eula being there."

Her mother stopped typing and eyed Ruby. She picked up a clip from the table, gathered up her long brown hair, and snapped it into place on the back of her head. She reached over the typewriter to a plate of fried zucchini sticks and helped herself to one.

"I asked you to check on her since she doesn't have your grandmother to help her. Just see how she's doing, that's all. She is your great-aunt, after all."

"I've got too much to do."

"*What* do you have to do?"

"I'm plotting my revenge on Melba. I thought about tying her to an anthill..."

"Let this go, Ruby. You and Melba—"

"I can't let it go, Mama. She's like a pesky mosquito. When I see her, I wanna slap her before she has a chance to bite me."

"Ruby! What a thing to say! Listen to me. Remember how upset you were when your grandpa died last year? Ruby, two people died in that accident—Melba lost her father. Can you imagine how sad she must be?"

Ruby's stomach clenched. "Sad people don't pick on other people."

"Sometimes they do. We can't know Melba's reasons. Probably she doesn't know them herself."

Ruby sucked in her breath. Melba knew. "I don't want to talk about it. I just want her to leave me alone."

"Time will help. You won't see much of her this summer, with her mama running the beauty shop full-time, and Melba watching the little ones."

Ruby thought about summer. Summer meant operetta in Halleluia.

"It's too bad she's a Methodist. If she was a Baptist, I wouldn't have to see her on Sundays, either. Remember last week at church when we stood up to sing the last hymn, and she screeched louder than train brakes?"

Ruby's mother pressed her fingers to her mouth, but Ruby could see her eyes laughing.

"Well, Voxie Varnado told me after church that Melba said she had to practice like that, to get ready for this year's operetta, to make sure she had the kids' lead. She always gets to be the kid star anyway. I don't know why anybody else under twelve bothers to audition." Ruby pushed her hair out of her face. "I wish Miss Eula were here. She'd know what to say about Melba Jane."

Ruby's mother pulled Ruby to her and hugged her hard. "I surely wish she was, too. Why don't you write her about it and see what she says? Then you can go to the post office and mail all of today's letters, and pop in and say hi to Miss Mattie for me. You need chicken feed, too."

"I know. But Miss Mattie is such a crab."

"She has a lot on her mind, sweetie. Will you go for me? I've got to get this column finished before the end of the afternoon."

Ruby sighed. She helped herself to a slice of zucchini bread.

"Kiss me," said her mother.

Ruby did.

"It'll all work out, I promise."

Ruby rolled her eyes at her mother and headed for the back door.

Her mother smiled and called after Ruby. "I hear that Peterson's Egg Ranch has been sold. Ask Miss Mattie if she knows the particulars, would you? And don't forget to check the mail!"

The knothole had never looked so empty. Box 72 was empty, too. Miss Dot, the postmistress, smiled at Ruby. "There's still another truck delivery to come in, honey. I bet today is the day."

"Yes, ma'am," said Ruby, and she smiled back, but she was worried. She hadn't had one letter, not one. Maybe Miss Eula had already forgotten her. Then she remembered what her mama had said: "Nobody's had a letter yet, Ruby. Give Miss Eula time to step off the plane!"

She sighed and mailed the four letters she'd written that afternoon and walked to Miss Mattie's store, where Miss Mattie handed her a broom and pointed. Ruby swept the wooden floors and filled the cracker barrel and listened to customers talk about bunions and the too-hot weather. As she finished her string of chores and tried to hang the broom on its peg in the back room, Miss Mattie towered over her. "What could be better than a good job to take your mind off your troubles?" Before Ruby could answer, she added, "You come see me again on Friday."

That was that. It sounded definite, done, over.

Miss Mattie strode away to wait on a customer. Ruby gave a heavy sigh and walked toward the back door. Standing outside, with her face pressed against the screen, was Melba Jane. She had three small Lathams hanging on to her legs.

Ruby sucked in her breath. "What are *you* doing here?"

Melba Jane sniffed. "It's a free country. It's none of your beeswax why I'm here." Melba's formerly straight hair now fell in a mass of ringlets around her face. She shook them at Ruby.

"What's the matter with your head?"

"Nothing! It's a new hairdo. *Sprayed* magazine says it's the latest look."

"It looks like you stuck your finger in a light socket."

"It does not! I take time with my looks, unlike *some* people."

Melba's littlest sister pulled on Melba's shorts. "Ice pop!"

"In a minute, Violet!"

Ruby pushed her unruly hair out of her face with both hands. Melba watched her carefully through the screen door. "For instance," she sneered, "look at those hands! Your nails are…disgraceful! I bet your palms are full of calluses, from all that ball playing and tree climbing you do. Really, Ruby, it's sooo unladylike."

Ruby's neck grew hot and a bad taste rose in her mouth, but she remembered Miss Eula's advice. "You know what, Melba Jane? You just wish you had a life half as interesting as mine—that's what's wrong with you. I'm going to ignore you, even though you are so full of it, if you were a tick, you'd burst. I'm ignoring you. Now go away."

"Ha! You wish! What an exciting life you lead! Sweeping floors for Miss Mattie!" Melba opened the screen door and jeered at Ruby. "And now your dear, sweet grandmother is gone, and you don't have anybody left to hide behind and pretend everything is peachy-fine."

Ruby's face colored. Her heart beat hard in her chest. With a short, hard shove, she pushed past Melba Jane and walked stiffly toward her silver maple.

"You keep your ugly hands off me!" yelled Melba Jane. "You'll be sorry! Hey! Come back here, you chicken!"

Ruby kept walking. She held her arms stiffly at her sides, her hands clenched into fists. "Ignore her." She pictured Melba as a fat balloon with ringlets, rising into the air and floating away.

"*Bwauck-bwauck-bwauck!*" Melba's sisters began *bwaucking* along with her. Ruby kept walking. "*Bwauck-bwauck-bwauck!*"

"I *can't* ignore her!" Ruby wheeled, but Melba had shooed herself and her sisters into the mercantile, so Ruby shouted after her. "*You're* the chicken! You don't even know *how* to climb a tree!" But she knew no one heard her.

Ruby reached her silver maple and gave it a little pat. She had climbed it a hundred times, and now she did again. She leaned into a wide **V** in the branches and closed her eyes, and soon her heart slowed to its regular rhythm and she even felt drowsy. She looked up through the leaves at patches of clear sky…the same sky Miss Eula said she would be under, right now. It didn't feel like it. She climbed down her tree and looked in the knothole, out of habit. *No mail.* She decided to try the post office one more time before she walked home.

Dear Ruby, Ruby, Ruby!

Aloha! Aloha means hello AND good-bye in Hawaiian. Aloha-hello! I am here!

The plane taxied onto the runway. I walked out of it. Flowers, flowers, flowers! People, people, people! calling "Aloha!" and putting leis around my neck and kissing me on the cheek. Pretty soon, I had flower necklaces up to my lips! They smelled like heaven. I will send you a picture.

It WAS heaven to see Johnson, Annette, and the baby, who still doesn't have a name. She is adorable, Ruby. You will love your new cousin. She was wearing a muumuu—just like the ones Johnson has sent me, only smaller, of course.

Everyone here wears flip-flops or goes BARE-FOOT!

I will write more later—we are going to a luau. I am going to dance the hula and eat poi. What is poi, you ask? Who knows! I'll find out and give you a report. I have not received any letters from you yet but I suspect, since it's only been two days, they are coming any moment now...I do miss you so.

> Love, love, love, and Aloha-good-bye!
> your (excited) grandmother,
> Miss Eula

June 14

Well, Good Garden of Peas, Miss Happiness,

Your letter was exciting. I was depressed at first. I was sure you would hate Hawaii. Maybe by now you do.

For your information, Melba Jane is curling her hair so loopy it looks like a heap of catfish guts. It's very attractive. I told her so.

I read your letter to the chickens. Then I read them from "anchovy" to "angel" in the dictionary. Ivy has asked me for a bedtime story every night, since she is egg sitting. "No violence," she said.

I am sweeping floors for Miss Mattie. It is total torture.

Every time I walk past our silver maple tree, I feel like an empty paper bag.

Here is another picture of me.

Free advice: Don't eat anything called poi.

Love,
your (awfully lonesome) granddaughter,
Ruby L.

Pee Ess: Someone is buying Peterson's Egg Ranch!

Dear Wasting Away,

I received the ten letters you sent me the day I left! What a lucky number! But my goodness, I hope you have pulled out of your WOE IS ME.

Ruby, Hawaii is COLORFUL. There are acres of sugarcane growing here! No cotton. Pineapples, too! Along the side of the road there are pineapple stands. You pay ten cents for a slice, cut fresh. The juice runs down your arm and chin.

The baby is two months old today and finally has a name: Leilani. It means Flower of Heaven, in Hawaiian. She looks me in the eye and says, "Thhhwwaaaaagh!" A genius, of course.

I walked yesterday on a sugar-sand beach. It was so soft, Ruby. Not like the rough shore around Lake Jasper. And the waves! "Come and play," they sang. So I did. I jumped in. My muumuu mushroomed around me. No one even noticed! Here, everyone jumps into the waves!

I feel like I've always belonged here. There are even pink houses. Lots of pink here. But no you. I do miss you.

>Love and Aloha,
>your (content) grandmother,
>Miss Eula

June 19

Dear Too Happy,

Well, I don't think "Thhhwwaaaaagh!" is anything to write home about. I write full sentences. I write long letters. And what kind of a name is Leilani? Does she have a middle name? Maybe I can pronounce THAT.

For your information, I am sending you a paper I got in the mail from my next year's teacher. It is full of questions for me to answer. I am making a copy for you.

Melba Jane's hair looks worse by the day. I feel soooo sorry for her. At least she quit wearing those tappy shoes.

I am teaching the chickens to dance. Bemmie has two left feet. Bess steps on her all the time. Their favorite song is "Why Did You Leave Me, Miss Eula?"

Free advice: Mama says pineapple is NOT good for young babies, so don't give any to that kid. Try hot chili peppers. Or poi.

Love,
your (just trying to be helpful) granddaughter,
Ruby L.

Pee Ess: I can't believe we have a new teacher at Halleluia School. No one new comes here.

Welcome to Mr. Ishee's Fourth Grade!

In a few weeks, you will be entering fourth grade. I will be your teacher. I am new to Halleluia School, and I am looking forward to getting to know you. So we can become acquainted more quickly, please fill out this questionnaire and return it to me in the envelope I have enclosed. Have fun with your summer! I can't wait to meet you!

1. What is your full name?
   Ruby Garnet Lavender

2. Where do you live?
   I live right outside of Halleluia—in fact, I've measured it, and I live 1,347 steps from the schoolhouse. Or maybe that's 13,470, I can't remember, but either way that's a lot of steps when it's raining, believe me. Lots of kids live in Raz or Stringer or Montrose. It's too far to walk to see them, and I don't drive. Yet.

3. Tell me about your town or your neighborhood.
   There's nothing to tell. Miss Eula Dapplevine was the only colorful thing about Halleluia, and she up and left for Hawaii, deserting her kin (me), not to mention her chickens.

4. Tell me about your family.

Miss Eula is my grandmother. I had a grandfather. He died. So Miss Eula went to Hawaii. I
have a father but I do not know him. He left
Halleluia before I was born, but my mama
didn't go anywhere. My mama is the first
woman in Aurora County to be the county extension agent for home and garden. She is
always in someone's garden or kitchen, or at
the typewriter, or on the telephone. People
call her with questions like "How long do I
let my canned beans boil so they aren't
poisonous?"

5. Tell me about yourself.

I am a chicken thief. And a housepainter. And a
floor sweeper. I have red hair and freckles the
color of new pennies. I am a good writer. I
have three chickens: Ivy, Bemmie, and Bess. I
am about to have three more because Ivy laid
three eggs. I do not eat meat.

6. What do you do in your spare time?

I am totally tortured sweeping floors at Miss
Mattie's mercantile. I USED to have a fun life, until
my grandmother up and left me for some baby.

7. **What are your favorite subjects in school?**
   I never think about school in the summer. It is bad luck. Ask me in September.

8. **What do you plan to do with your summer?**
   Do you have any suggestions for a tortured nine-year-old? I <u>will not</u> go to Vacation Bible School over in Bay Springs, or to Camp Walkaway. That's just organized torture.

9. **What else would you like to tell me?**
   Since you are new here, I do not want to scare you. So I will not mention that the (always) star of every year's operetta has catfish gut hair. And guess what? She's in the fourth grade this year! Lucky you.

   Free advice: Folks here are nice but nosy. Keep your front room picked up. Always keep a fresh pitcher of sweet iced tea in your refrigerator.

Dear Miss Eula the Hard-hearted,

Only six more days to baby chicks!! Bemmie is bossy and argues with Bess. Ivy ignores them and keeps nesting. Bemmie says to Ivy, "You could at least give us a peek!"

This week I have read the "B" words in the dictionary. I have told them stories... their favorite is "Rubylocks and the Three Chickens." Starting June 25, I am sleeping in the chicken house to make sure I don't miss anything.

For your information, I am still sweeping floors for Miss Mattie. It is still torture.

Here is another picture of me. I am two months old in this picture.

Melba Jane looked so bad today, the dogcatcher took her to the pound. He said, "I thought she was a Saint Bernard."

Free advice: It is worth a trip to Halleluia to see miracle chickens born.

Love,

your (about to be busy) granddaughter,

Ruby L.

Pee Ess: Guess what? A <u>family</u> is buying Peterson's Egg Ranch. That means kids. I don't know how many yet.

Dear Ruby darlin;

We have traveled to the "Big Island," called Hawaii. I am going to walk across a volcano today! It is inactive, and folks walk across it every day. Imagine!

I made grass skirts for me and Leilani. She looks cute in hers. I look like a grandmother in mine. My favorite hula song is "Lovely Hula Hands." My hands are awfully knobby, but they are lovely when I do the hula.

Here are my first photographs. Just look at us! I bet you hardly recognize your uncle Johnson. He's the tall, handsome one. Do you like my hat? I made it myself, from palm leaves. Here are post-cards, too. My favorite is the one of a volcano erupting.

Did you know kings and queens used to rule Hawaii?

How _are_ you? What is going on with Melba Jane? What is happening at the egg ranch? Your mama wrote me that it was for sale. I hope someone with children buys the place.

> Love,
> your (tropical) grandmother,
> Miss Eula

Dear Ruby Lavender,

My name is Ferrell Ishee. I am the new fourth-grade teacher in Halleluia. I read your questionnaire with great interest. I have a niece who is nine years old and visiting from Memphis who would love to meet you. So would my wife and I.

We are making root-beer floats the day after tomorrow at 4 p.m. to celebrate our move to the old egg-ranch property. Please come if you can.

With much anticipation,
Ferrell Ishee

Dear Miss Grass Skirt,
  For your information:

1. I am going to Peterson's Egg Ranch this afternoon to meet the Ishees and have root-beer floats. There's a kid my age! I'll give you a report.

2. Melba Jane hasn't been able to leave the dog pound. No one will claim her. Too bad.

3. Old Mr. Peterson moved in with his son, Young Mr. Peterson, over in Raleigh. He told Miss Mattie that he hoped you stayed and stayed in Hawaii. Ha! You aren't thinking of doing that, are you?

4. Chicken update: Ivy stays put on her eggs so much I am afraid she doesn't eat or drink. I ask her if she's hungry and she says, "Nothing for me, thank you." I pick her up every day at least once and take her to her food. Then I have to fight Bemmie, who tries to get into Ivy's nest. As soon as Ivy eats, she gets back on her nest. I have watched her turn the eggs.

She turns them with her feet many times a day. She will be a good mother. I love the chicks already.

My hand is tired of writing! I have to go have a root-beer float!
>
> Love,
> your (expectant) granddaughter,
> Ruby L.

Pee Ess: What is it like to walk on a volcano?

8

June 23

The sun winked off Ruby's bike in the four o'clock light of afternoon. She pedaled onto the egg-ranch property, toward the big white house with the wrap-around porch. Far away she heard the rumble of thunder. She was so hot her clothes stuck to her. She licked her lips. Salty. A root-beer float would be perfect today.

The long open-sided laying sheds were empty now. Beyond them was the tin-roofed house. It was surrounded by lemon lilies and a picket fence. Ruby leaned her bike against the fence. She heard music coming from the house, and a shout. "Yeeee-haaaa! Swing your partner!"

Ruby tiptoed up the path to the front screen door and peered in. There in the front room danced a tall, round man with a full beard. In his arms he held a very plain, very heavy woman who was laughing from the bottom of her belly. The big man laughed along with her. Their dancing shook the floor.

"Good garden of peas!" exclaimed Ruby.

"That's Uncle Tater and Aunt Tot."

Ruby whirled. "You scared me half to death!" In front of her stood a girl with enormous blue eyes and peaks of short white hair, like meringue on a lemon icebox pie.

"Sorry!"

"Where's Mr. Ishee?"

"That's him. We call him Uncle Tater. Aunt Tot's real name is Cornelia, but nobody calls her that. You'll get used to them; they're wonderfully nice. They're going to have a baby in October. I'm staying with them for the summer, helping them move in. I've done a study on them. I love your overalls— they go so nicely with your short-sleeve shirt and no shoes. You're Ruby, right?"

Ruby swallowed. "Good garden of peas."

"That's a great name. Can I call you Peas for short?"

Ruby scrunched her eyebrows. "I guess so."

"Oh, good. We've already got a secret together."

Ruby studied the girl. She was wearing a light brown shirt with square front pockets. Brown shorts with deep side pockets. Brown boots with long laces. White socks that stuck up from the boot tops. A brown hat hung on her back. It was hard, with a domed top and a leather string through it, to keep it around her neck. She wore a pocket watch on her belt loop. She was brown and white all over.

"Are you going on a trip to the jungle or something?" Ruby couldn't guess.

The girl pulled a pencil out from behind her ear and reached into one of the shorts' big pockets and pulled out a spiral-topped notebook. She moved to the porch railing. "I'm an anthropologist."

"A what?"

"An anthropologist. I study people. Do you know Margaret Mead?"

"No. Does she live in Memphis?"

"Margaret Mead! Margaret Mead! She was an anthropologist. Famous! She studied people. Tape-recorded them. Made notes. Wrote books."

"Why?"

"To find out why people do what they do."

"Why?"

"It's important! It explains human beings. We're all different and we're all the same—that's what Margaret Mead said. And I'm going to be just like her and travel all over the world and study people."

Ruby pulled on her earlobe and narrowed her eyes. "Who are you?"

"I'm Helen Dove Ishee, but folks call me Dove. My grandmother's name was Helen. She died right before I was born."

"I still have a grandma. Sort of."

Dove gave Ruby a questioning look. Inside the house the music had stopped, but the dancing continued. Ruby heard the farm report now on the radio. Mr. Ishee and his wife were dancing to the farm report.

Ruby explained. "My grandma—she's on a trip; she's not here right now. But I have chickens, and eggs about to hatch."

"Wow! I wish I could see that."

Ruby felt important. "I'm sleeping with the chickens starting next week, so I can make sure to watch the chicks hatch. You can come if you want."

"Really? You mean it?"

Ruby caught herself. She didn't mean it at all.

Dove plowed ahead. "That's great! Can I bring my equipment?"

Mr. Ishee and his wife danced into the screen door. It whipped open, and they were suddenly on the porch, doing a last twirl. Ruby sidestepped them just in time, and Dove laughed.

"You are Ruby, I bet." Mr. Ishee was bent over with his hands on his knees, breathing hard. "Look at that ruby-red hair."

Ruby's hair slopped out of its ponytail. Great wisps of it trailed all along her shoulders and face. She brushed it back with a dusty hand. "Yep, it's me. Are you the new teacher?"

"You bet I am. Come on in! Come on in!" He motioned everyone inside, while gazing adoringly toward the woman he had been dancing with. "And this is my dear wife, Tot."

Tot was trying to catch her breath. Her face was as red as Ruby's hair. She smiled and gave a weak wave. "Bless your heart. Bless your heart."

Dove grinned at Ruby. "See? Nice as pie. Come on. Let's have some ice cream."

"How do you take your root-beer floats, Ruby?" Uncle Tater/Mr. Ishee pulled two half-gallons of Blue Bell ice cream from the freezer. "Vanilla or chocolate?"

"Vanilla." Ruby had dodged dozens of half-unpacked boxes as she'd followed Dove to the kitchen. The front-room couch was piled high with books. Clothes draped the back of every chair. The walls were covered with the ugliest paintings Ruby had ever seen and more leaned against the walls. The kitchen counter was lined with geraniums growing in Chock full o' Nuts coffee cans.

"Good garden of peas! Y'all had a tornado go through here."

Tot laughed her belly laugh. "That's what moving will do for you." She bent over, rummaged through a tall box, then stood up, puffing, and pulled an ice-cream scoop with her. "Here it is, sweetheart!"

Mr. Ishee took the scoop from his wife and planted a long kiss on her large lips. "Leave it to Tot to find what I can't see." He sledded the scoop through the ice cream. "Tot, did we think to buy root beer?"

Tot patted her husband's bearded face with a meaty hand. "It's in one of these Winn-Dixie bags here, somewhere."

Dove was already looking. "Here it is, Aunt Tot."

"Oh, good. Bless your heart, Dove. Bless your heart."

Mr. Ishee stood with the ice-cream scoop dripping full of vanilla ice cream. "Do we have glasses, Tot?"

Tot laughed again. "Somewhere! Let's see, which box?"

Ruby moved a stack of *National Geographic*s from a kitchen chair. "Here's some bowls…"

"Bowls! That'll do!" They made root-beer floats in red plastic bowls and sat on the porch, with spoons and straws. Ruby listened to Dove's aunt and uncle complete each other's sentences and remembered, *Miss Eula and Grandpa Garnet used to do that.*

"…and I'm invited to spend the night with Ruby already!" Dove was talking about the chickens.

"Well, bless your heart!" Tot said to Ruby. "Bless your heart. You surely know how to make a body feel welcome."

Mr. Ishee peered, squinch-eyed, into the distance. "Who in the world is coming? Tot, is somebody else supposed to be coming?" A rooster-tail of dust swirled around a green pickup truck turning into the ranch. Old Ezra Jackson's truck. It rattled up the lane to the house, stopped in front of the picket fence, and the passenger door opened. Gingerly, someone stepped out with a package and waved thanks to Old Ezra. Ezra tipped his hat at everyone and drove off in another powdery cloud. His passenger posed, hand on hip, and smiled. The others on the porch wouldn't know her, but Ruby did.

Her heart sank. Melba Jane.

9

No one moved. Ruby was struck speechless. Melba's hair was curled into a mass of catfish guts even loopier than before. Her lips were painted a brilliant red. She was licked to a gloss in a poofy scarlet dress, shiny black shoes, and enough bangle bracelets on her wrists to sound like a tiny band.

"Can we help you?" Mr. Ishee looked worried.

Melba sashayed to the porch, sweetly smiling, and put a gloved hand to her cheek.

"Oh! I'm *so sorry*! I didn't *realize* you had *company*! I was just stopping by to be neighborly. I can come back another time."

Ruby opened her mouth, but nothing came out.

Tot beamed. "We wouldn't hear of it! We love company! How lovely of you to welcome us to

Halleluia, bless your heart. We're the Ishees from Memphis. Tell us who you are, dear."

"I'm Melba Jane Latham, thank you. My mama runs the beauty shop in town, Locks by Leila. If you need your hair done, you just come to our house. We have the most hairdo books in the county and all the latest movie magazines to read while you're under the dryer."

Tot patted at her straight-as-straw hair and smiled. "Come on up here, sweetheart, and let us get a good look at you. That's a stunning outfit. I believe you're in Mr. Ishee's class this September. I remember your name."

"I don't want to interrupt..." Melba gave Ruby a cool stare.

"Another student of mine!" Mr. Ishee came to life finally. "Come, come! Do stay and let's get acquainted. We were just enjoying root-beer floats on this sweltering day. I'm sure you know Ruby."

"Oh, yes, sir. I *know* Ruby." Melba raised an eyebrow at Ruby. "Hello, Ruby."

"Hey," Ruby managed to croak.

"This is our niece, Dove. She's staying with us for the summer," said Aunt Tot.

"Yes, ma'am! I heard that at the beauty shop. I brought this present for you, Dove."

Dove clapped her mouth shut. Then she opened it and blurted, "You would be *great* for my studies. Can I tape-record you?"

"Certainly. I have a wonderful voice."

Ruby blinked.

Dove opened the present as everyone looked on. Inside was a handmade flyer:

COUPON!

Good for ONE
Shampoo and Supper Anytime
at Locks by Leila

Tot touched her fingertips to her chest. "How very sweet!"

Dove giggled with delight. "Thanks!"

Tot waded to her feet. "Let's get our new guest a float, sweetheart. These girls can keep each other company while we do." She pulled at her husband's sleeve, and the two of them left the porch.

Ruby sat cross-legged on a porch rocker and watched Dove, whose blue eyes were transfixed, mesmerized by Melba Jane, the walking beauty shop. Ruby felt a stab of jealousy that made her wince.

"This is great!" Dove had her notebook out, her

pencil poised. "I'm going to write all of this in my book."

Ruby tried to pull Dove's attention away from Melba. "What's that book for?"

"I keep track of my studies in here," said Dove. She explained to Melba: "I study people, just like Margaret Mead did. When I'm grown up, I'm going to Fiji and Africa and Las Vegas to study people there." She looked at both girls. "I'll get lots of practice here. A whole new town of people to practice on! I'm just about practiced-out in Memphis, or at least that's what my mama says."

"I'm good to practice on. What do you want to know? I'll tell you *everything.*" Melba gave Ruby a brick-hard stare, and Ruby looked away.

"I'll interview you first, Melba Jane. Then who?"

"I'm the most interesting," said Melba. Ruby rolled her eyes.

Dove scribbled in her notebook. "I need the whole town. That's how you find out why people in a certain place do what they do. So, I'll interview everybody in Halleluia. I'll learn about the town excitements and tragedies, and customs and traditions, and then I'll write it all up, and say, 'The Halleluians act *this* way, and here's why.' But first I have to know all the facts. For instance, what's the biggest thing that ever happened in this town?"

Ruby's face grew hot. She wanted off the porch. "I'm going to help make the floats."

Melba planted herself in front of Ruby's rocker. Her voice was sweetly polite, but her face was a sneer for Ruby only. "What's the matter, Ruby? You don't want to talk about the biggest thing that ever happened here? Why not?"

Dove jumped up. "Wait. Let me get my tape recorder and my camera. I'll be right back." She disappeared into the house, and Ruby and Melba were alone. Dark clouds had been drifting over the porch, and the old chicken yard was in shade. A new wind whooshed through the trees, fluffing the leaves and stirring the dust.

Ruby hitched up her left overalls strap. "I'm going home. We're fixin' to get wet out here."

Melba pressed her lips together and popped them apart. "Go ahead. I don't need you here to have fun with your new friend."

Ruby gritted her teeth. "You think it's *fun*, talking about...talking about..."

"The accident? I wonder how much of it I should tell. I bet your new friend Dove would *love* to hear all about it."

Ruby's heart began to skip in her chest. Aunt Tot appeared in the doorway, her arms full of float. "Here, Ruby, help me with the door." Dove appeared with her tape recorder in her hands and her camera slung around her shoulder. She had put on her hat. "Here's my equipment." Behind her came her uncle, carrying a kitchen chair. "Here you go, Melba."

"Why, thank you." Melba used the most syrupy voice Ruby had ever heard. She arranged herself daintily in the chair and with her pinky finger pointed to Dove's tape recorder. "Is it on?"

Dove thumped herself into a chair next to Melba and pushed a button. "Yep, it's on. I put new batteries in yesterday." She cleared her throat. "It's June twenty-third, and this is going to be Melba Jane Latham talking about the biggest event ever in Halleluia, Mississippi. Melba Jane, are you ready?"

Melba held up her hand in a stop sign, while she took a long sip of root-beer float. Ruby edged toward the wide porch steps. Uncle Tater and Aunt Tot sat next to each other in the porch swing and held hands. A gusty breeze turned the weathervane on the old chicken house, and the sweet scent of rain danced on the dust.

Ruby stepped down a step. "My mama's expecting

me home about now." Her heart made a pounding sound in her ears.

"Don't go yet, Ruby," said Melba, a whine in her voice. "I know you want to hear my story." Melba smoothed her poofy dress across her thighs.

"Do you really have to go, Ruby?" asked Aunt Tot. "Can I call your mother and ask her if you can stay awhile longer? Wouldn't you like to stay awhile longer?"

"No, ma'am. I have to go. I mean, yes, ma'am, I'd love to stay, but no, ma'am, I can't. I mean, I need to go home."

"She means," said Melba Jane with a short sniff, "she means, she doesn't *want* to hear this story, isn't that right, Ruby?" Melba snatched the microphone from Dove and, with her too-red lips, began: "This story, this biggest thing ever that happened in Halleluia, Mississippi, this is the story of how my daddy died—drowned to *death*!—last summer in Lake Jasper."

10

"Good glory!" Tot grabbed Tater's arm. "You don't mean to say!"

Dove turned white. Her uncle vaulted out of the swing, and Tot clung to the chain to steady herself. "Well!" said Mr. Ishee. "This is turning out to be quite the day. I don't think a story like this is suitable for Tot, in her delicate condition." Thunder rumbled far away. Ruby's heart skittered into her throat.

"Do sit down, Tater darlin'." Tot released the chain and held out her hands to her husband. "I'm fine, fine. You know I'm as strong as a horse. Go on, Melba, if you can, sweetheart. Do you want some water?"

Melba cleared her throat delicately. "No, ma'am, thank you."

Ruby cast a desperate look at the sky and stepped

down another step. "It's getting downright windy out here. I'm going home before the rain hits." No one heard her.

"It was last summer." Melba's voice was even and strong, like she had rehearsed these sentences a thousand times, and in spite of her resolve to leave, Ruby listened. "My daddy and Ruby's granddaddy drove to Raleigh together to a Grange meeting. It was the biggest one of the year and lasted all day and part of the night. They were *supposed* to stay in Raleigh for the night and come home the next morning, but they didn't. They started for home, but they didn't come home, either. The next morning Mr. Harvey Popham found the car. Ruby's granddaddy had driven them right off the Lake Jasper bridge and into the water. Everybody says he fell asleep. They were still in the car."

Silence. Ruby couldn't go now. "It was an accident." She spoke quietly and stared at her bare feet.

Melba held her chin high. "Some say that. Some don't."

Ruby sucked in her breath and met Melba's eyes. "It was an accident."

"Maybe." Melba turned to face Ruby. "But it never had to happen, did it?" Ruby pulled on her earlobe and felt the sweat beading on her upper lip. Now Melba was out of her chair and standing on the step in front of Ruby. "You want me to tell more?"

"I want you to shut up," said Ruby evenly. Her stomach twisted itself into a knot.

"Girls..." Tot pushed herself up and out of the swing.

Melba hissed into Ruby's face. "I can tell plenty more!"

"Shut up, Melba Jane!" Ruby heard her heartbeat: *run-away-run-away-run-away!*

Mr. Ishee helped his wife to her feet and stood with her. Dove sat, still as a stick.

Melba Jane's eyes were mean and bright, and her face was smack in front of Ruby's. She spoke in a low snarl, so only Ruby could hear. "I can tell whatever I want to tell, and you can't make me shut up. You can only listen, Ruby Lavender, so why don't *you* shut up, and just *listen*, while I tell *everything* about last summer's accident!" Melba grabbed Ruby's arm and gave it a vicious yank. "Sit down!"

Ruby jerked her arm away from Melba's grasp and was down the stairs, racing for her bicycle. Her heart slammed against her rib cage. She tripped and fell. She pushed herself up with scraped hands and kept running. A downdraft roared in under the trees and through the chicken yard, bringing the rain with it.

She reached her bike just as a *boom!* of thunder crashed above her and the sky opened. Rain fell so hard it washed over Ruby like a river. It plastered her hair against her face, but still she jerked her bike away from the fence and felt her way onto the seat, slicking her hair back with one hand and holding the handlebars of her bike with the other. All she could see was the rain, like a white sheet all around her. The sound filled her ears and seemed to yell *hurry-hurry-hurry!* And she did, wobbling crazily back and forth on her bike until she was sure of herself.

She heard a vague echoing from the porch. It was Tot, Mr. Ishee, Dove, shouting for her to wait. The wind pushed her on, *this-way-this-way,* and her legs pedaled through the storm as fast as they could take her.

June 23

Dear Miss Eula,

I was so upset in my last letter, I forgot to tell you the details.

Mr. Ishee has a wife and a niece. The niece is Dove. She is in the fourth grade, like me, and she is visiting for the summer. She is from Memphis. She wears strange clothes. She is an antthoo…no, an arthra… a studier of people who live in places and what they do there. I bet she knows all the secret stories about how bad Hawaii is.

Mama let me have chocolate pudding for dinner and said I didn't have to take a bath because I'd already had one, riding home in the rain. She wants me to get some sleep but I can't. It is pouring and pouring rain. When are you coming home?

For your information, Ivy is a sitting fool. Bemmie is mad at everyone. Bess eats all the time and tells Bemmie to shut up. I read tonight from "carnival" to "crab apple." That was a lot of reading, believe me.

Love,
your (most unfortunate) grandchild,
Ruby L.

Pee Ess: How is Hortense?

Dear Ruby,

A family is buying Peterson's? How exciting!
Tell me everything—but then, I bet you already
did, and our letters are crisscrossing, like they
always do, Somewhere Over the Pacific. That's like
Somewhere Over the Rainbow, but wetter. Ha!

Ruby, I've been thinking, and I want to ask you
a favor. On August 1, it will be one year since your
grandpa died. I don't expect I'll be there, but it's
been on my mind for many months now, long
before I left for Hawaii, to do something special
on that day to remember him. Before I left on
my trip, I thought I would go to the cemetery on
August 1, maybe, and set out a nice meal for your
grandpa, maybe some fried chicken and coleslaw
and potato salad. Since he wouldn't actually EAT
what I brought, I had thought to take you with
me and have a picnic, and just chat with Garnet.
Now I won't be there, and I don't expect a picnic
all by yourself is much fun...but I'd still like to do
something. Maybe you could cut a bunch of
black-eyed Susans from your grandpa's flower
bed and leave them on his grave from me and
you?

Don't do this if you don't want to. And any day
is fine—it doesn't have to be THE day. Just a
remembrance to mark the fact that Garnet was in

this world, and that the world was a good place because he was here.

We are about to go to a famous waterfall and watch people dive from high up on the rocks into the river below! Everybody does it! Do you think I should try this, too? Your uncle Johnson says, "Not on your life!" Hmmph!

I miss you and miss you and miss you, and have only one other thing to tell you before I send this off: Your cousin Leilani is going to have RED HAIR! She looks so much like you, Ruby. Did you get my pictures?

> Love,
> your pretty good diver for a grandmother,
> Miss Eula

Aurora County News

Morning Edition, June 23

Operetta to Be Presented

The Town Operetta will be presented on August 1. This year's presentation (as reported earlier) will be "How Dear to My Heart Are the Scenes of My Childhood."

Main singing and acting parts will be assigned by audition. There will be a small chorus. Auditions will be held on June 25, at Halleluia School.

Please bring your own sheet music. A stage crew is also needed. Contact the director of this year's operetta (as usual) Miss Mattie Perkins, or show up at auditions. Our (usual) art and scenery director, Miss Eula Dapplevine, is still in Hawaii. Mrs. Ferrell Ishee ("call me Tot") has volunteered to help with art direction.

11

June 24

Ruby spent the morning with her chickens. Her mother was in Rose Hill, doing a home demonstration: "Freeze or Can Your Produce: Which One Is Right for You?" She had tried to get Ruby to go, but Ruby wanted to be home.

It had rained all night, and the dust that had swirled around everything was gone. The flowers surrounding the Pink Palace looked like they had been washed clean and put out to drip-dry. Ruby loved how fresh the earth smelled after a good rain. It was cooler, too. She sat on the back steps of the Pink Palace and watched Bemmie and Bess in the chicken yard, hunting for bugs near the butter-bean vine.

"Hey, Peas." Ruby turned to look in the direction of the voice. Dove came around the corner of the house.

"Hey, yourself." Ruby scratched a mosquito bite on her elbow and glowered at Dove.

"I met your aunt Mattie in the mercantile this morning. She told me you'd be here."

"Here I am."

Dove had a foil-covered plate with her. "This place is really pink!"

Ruby's face lightened. "You like it?"

"Oh, yeah. It's great!" Dove held out her plate and spoke in a coaxing voice. "Here. These are from Aunt Tot. They're cookies. She was worried about you. Me, too."

"Thanks." Ruby put the plate on the porch and gave Dove a what-do-you-want look.

Dove scratched the side of her face. "You and Melba aren't friends, are you?"

"Nope." Ruby went back to her elbow.

"She never did finish her story. Her mama—she's real nice—showed up to get her, because she had seen the rain coming."

Ruby shrugged and looked out at the chicken yard. Bemmie and Bess had gone into the chicken house. She had to make sure Bemmie wasn't picking on Ivy. She picked up a bucket full of corn and changed the subject. "Want to feed the chickens?"

Dove gave her a bright look, like a bird with a meringue-tipped head. "Sure!"

Ruby walked to the chicken yard and Dove followed her. "In that glass house?" The sun glinted off the greenhouse windows. "Is that where they live?" Dove was wearing the same thing she had worn the day before, the brown outfit with the boots and white socks. Her hat hung on her back and a pencil stuck up from behind her ear.

Ruby reached the gate. An enormous bed of black-eyed Susans grew next to it. The flowers brushed against the latch, and Ruby moved them out of her way. "This is the place."

"Your aunt Mattie told me about Miss Eula and how she went to Hawaii. Aunt Tot bought some paint and asked her all about the accident, too. It sounded terrible. I know why you didn't want to hear that story; it's just so sad…"

Ruby winced. "Yeah, it's sad." She opened the gate and Bess charged Ruby, squawking all the way. "Hey! I got it right here! Stop that!" Ruby tossed a handful of kernels to the back of the chicken yard, and Bess screeched after them. Bemmie tottled outside. Dove's face broke into a gleeful smile at the sight of the chickens. She clapped her hands together once and tucked them under her chin.

"No Ivy," said Ruby. "I'll have to make her eat again."

Dove made conversation. "Does your grand-mother say when she's coming back?"

Ruby waved a bumblebee away from her head. "No. She goes on and on about waterfalls and hula dancing and that drooling baby."

"Did you know there's a black sand beach in Hawaii? The sand is volcano ashes."

"Who cares?" Ruby hung the bucket on a hook.

"I care. Hawaiian people are interesting. I'm going to go there one day. I hope your grandmother comes back before the end of summer so I can interview her."

"Just don't interview me, Dove. I don't want to be interviewed by you, ever."

Dove slid her hands into her pockets and looked at the greenhouse. Some of the windows were open, and a breeze rattled the screens. "Aunt Tot says there are operetta auditions the day after tomorrow. She's helping with the scenery."

"Ha!" Ruby wiped her hands on her overalls. "Let me tell you about the operetta. Miss Mattie always directs it, so there goes any fun. Melba Jane always gets the starring kid role, so why bother to show up?"

"They need stagehands. That's what I want to do."

"Suit yourself." Bemmie and Bess tussled over the corn. They sounded like two old women screaming at each other.

"I don't want to go by myself. Want to go with me?"

Ruby thought about this. If she didn't offer to go with her, she knew Melba would. If she worked backstage, she might never have to see Melba. Or at least, Melba wouldn't see her.

"I'll think about it—"

"Good! Thanks."

"—just to see how it is without Miss Eula. She'll want to know." Ivy tiptoed out of the greenhouse. "Good garden of peas, Ivy! You must be hungry!" Bemmie made a beeline for Ivy's nest. "Oh, no you don't!" Ruby dashed for the greenhouse door and slapped it shut. Bemmie jumped and squawked.

"This is Bemmie!" grunted Ruby, using a knee to shove Bemmie away from the door. "She's jealous because Ivy has eggs to sit on and she doesn't." Ruby pointed to Bess. "And that one—she's a pig. She only looks like a chicken." She laughed at her own joke. "Her name is Bess."

Dove gave a little wave. "Hey, girls!"

Bemmie squawked and Bess gorged. "They're not impressed by company," Ruby said.

"They sure make a lot of noise."

"They calm down at night, when I read to them."

"You *read* to them?"

"Sure. It's calming. Come back tonight and I'll show you."

"Okay! What are you reading?"

"The dictionary."

"The dictionary! How do you read the dictionary?"

"How do you think? You just read it. There's a lot of weird words in the dictionary."

"I've got something better than that. I'll bring it tonight."

"They like the dictionary!"

The girls returned to the porch, where Ruby peeled the foil back from Aunt Tot's plate of cookies. She picked one up and studied it. It was as flat as a fingernail.

"I wouldn't eat it, if I were you. I think she forgot to add some stuff. Or she added too much stuff."

"Wow." Ruby raised her eyebrows and held the cookie over her head to get a look at it from the bottom. "I never saw anybody mess up a cookie like this."

"You should see her mashed potatoes. They look like glue and taste worse. But Uncle Tater loves everything she cooks. I eat lots of peanut butter and jelly."

"Come over and eat with me and Mama tonight, if you want. My mama's the best cook in the county."

Dove hesitated. "I'm invited to Melba's for supper."

"Oh." Ruby bristled and stalked into the Pink Palace, leaving the plate of cookies on the porch. "Have a nice time." She closed the door.

June 25

Dear Miss Hula Hands,

Last night Dove came to visit. She had been to Melba Jane's. They had been in her mother's makeup!

"Get that stuff off your face!" I told her. "You'll scare Ivy. She's sensitive." But she didn't, so we had to get used to looking at her like that.

Dove told Melba about the chicks. Melba said those eggs should have been somebody's breakfast. She's hateful. Dove tape-recorded the chickens. Bess tried to eat the microphone. Dove took pictures. Bemmie hogged the camera.

For your information, Dove brought over a book last night—THE HAWAIIAN ISLANDS AT A GLANCE. It put the chickens right to sleep. How can you stay awake over there?

Dove wants to tape-record Mama working. I told her to tape-record Mama cooking and take that tape to her aunt Tot.

> Love,
> your (depressed) grandchild,
> Ruby L.

Pee Ess: <u>Anthropologist</u>. Like Margaret Mead. Do you know her?

Dear Miss Eula—Miss Eula!

Good garden of peas! I just checked the chickens, and I can hear PEEPING from the eggs! PEEPING! The chicks are ready to hatch! Mama came to listen and she is amazed! I told her she is going to be a grandmother and she said, "That's what you think!" I've got to go tell Dove. I'm meeting her at the schoolhouse for the operetta tryouts. I am going to be on the scenery crew. Without you! Woe! And yay! for the chicks!

I have to go NOW!

Love,
your (excited!) granddaughter,
Ruby L.

Pee Ess: PEEEEEEEEEEPING!!

Dear Ruby,

This morning I received the copy you sent me of the questionnaire you filled out for school, and I must say it's as fine a masterpiece as you have ever written....I believe it would set world records in the Truth Stretchers Hall of Fame. But I must take exception to "Chicken Thief." You are not a chicken thief! You are a Chicken Liberator of the Highest Order. If I am ever a chicken and need liberating, I know just who to call.

Love,
your (fellow liberator) grandmother,
Miss Eula

12

June 25

Let's see." Ruby's mother stood barefoot in her kitchen, wrapping loaves of fig bread fresh from the oven. Her hair was in a braid down her back. She used her arm to wipe sweat from her forehead. "Will you take some of these loaves to Miss Mattie, Ruby, since you are going to the schoolhouse? I know she loves it, and I'm trying a new recipe."

Ruby frowned. "Will you write her a note, so I don't have to explain it to her?"

Her mother sighed. "I guess I can. Go get your wagon, and I'll scribble something for Miss Mattie."

Ruby came back with Bemmie in the wagon. Bemmie wore a bandanna collar with a ribbon tied to it and looped around the wagon slats.

"Heavens! Is she going with you?"

"She has to go. I don't trust her with Ivy. I'll keep her out of the way."

Ruby loaded the box of bread loaves into the wagon, next to Bemmie, who screeched, squawked, and acted like she had no room to move. Ruby patted her. "Hush now, you silly. You get to go on a field trip. You'll like it at the schoolhouse."

Evelyn Lavender slipped her feet into a pair of clogs. "I'll be at Peterson's Ranch while you're gone. I'm going to take some of this bread to Mr. Ishee and meet him."

Ruby waved. "Don't eat anything out there."

The wagon bumped and banged over the dirt road. Bemmie squawked in protest the whole way. Ruby sang to her. Honeybees played in the trumpet vines that lined the road.

The school was chock-full. Ruby pulled her wagon around back and parked it under a shady chinaberry tree. She squatted and looked Bemmie in the eye. "You wait here. I've got a delivery to make, then I'll bring you some water." Bemmie gave Ruby an outraged look and a loud squawk.

Ruby lifted the box of bread with a *humppph!* and walked into the open back door of the schoolhouse, the door nearest the stage. Coming in from the brilliant sunshine, she was instantly blind and cool. She stopped in the darkness of the hallway to let her eyes adjust.

She heard a piano playing—that would be Mrs. Varnado at the piano, so Voxie was probably there, too. She'd introduce her to Dove. As Ruby made her way through the hallway, she heard Melba Jane begin to sing. She could see Melba in her mind's eye, beating on her chest, falling to her knees, raising her hands to the skies, the way she always did when she was on stage. Sickening.

Ruby found Miss Mattie sitting in the aisle seat in the tenth row, a clipboard on her lap, listening intently to Melba. Four more listeners sat with her, each with pencils poised and clipboards ready.

Ruby put the box down in the darkened aisle and handed Miss Mattie the note from her mother. Miss Mattie read it and gave Ruby a Yes-yes-I-understand-thank-you-leave-me-alone-for-now-I'm-doing-important-work wave. Ruby nodded and walked back the way she had come, without even glancing at Melba Jane. Listening was bad enough.

She stopped at the girls' bathroom and took a mayonnaise lid out of her front overalls pocket and filled it with water. Then she walked into the brightness, shielding her eyes with her hand. "Here you go, Bemmie girl."

Ruby squinted. The wagon was empty. The ribbon and the bandanna lay limp on the ground. Bemmie was gone.

"Good garden of peas!" Ruby put the lid of water into the empty wagon. She hadn't the first notion how to go about looking for a runaway chicken. Should she go back the way she came? Maybe Bemmie was on her way back to the chicken yard, determined to get to Ivy's eggs.

She hardly had time to think about it before the screaming started. It came from inside the schoolhouse, a high-pitched scream followed by *"Get it off of meeeeeeeee!"* Melba.

13

Ruby raced inside the schoolhouse. She felt her way, tripping up the three back steps to the stage in the sudden darkness. In a panic, she slapped the heavy backstage curtain, trying to find an opening to the stage. The piano played *splank!-splink!-splunk! splank!-splink!-splunk!* over and over, down the scale, up the scale. Ruby crawled under the velvet curtain and stood up.

There was Bemmie, on the piano keys. Mrs. Varnado had plastered herself against the wall next to the piano and had squeezed her eyes shut.

The scenery crew rushed onstage. Tot's hands flew to her chest. Dove clutched a roll of construction paper and shouted to Melba. "It's okay! It's only a chicken! A chicken!" But Melba wasn't okay. She was hysterical.

Bemmie cocked her head, then jumped off the piano and raced for Melba, squawking with excitement, as if she'd found her long-lost, screaming mother. Melba's eyes popped as big as tea cakes. She ran.

Miss Mattie was on her feet. *"Get that chicken out of here!"* Melba stumbled past Ruby, smacked into the velvet curtain, and slid to the floor. Ruby lunged for Bemmie, but Bemmie scrabbled across Melba's back. Melba vaulted to her feet, upsetting a ladder. It toppled with a crash. Bemmie screamed and made a flying leap off the stage. Miss Mattie tried to swat her with her clipboard, but Bemmie veered and raced for the open back door of the schoolhouse and ran out.

Miss Mattie stomped up the front-stage stairs. Ruby stood with the others, looking at Melba Jane. Melba stood very still. She was silent, and she was blue. A can of paint had been on the top step of the ladder, and now, from her head to her toes, Melba was covered in it. Paint slid over her head like a peacock-blue silk scarf. It *drip, drip, drip*ped onto her shoulders, her nose, her crepe-paper dress, and her shiny red shoes.

No one spoke. The auditorium that had echoed with screeching and crashing just moments before was now as quiet as a grave.

"How *could* you bring that chicken in here?"

Miss Mattie's voice broke the silence, and suddenly everyone was talking at once, surrounding Melba Jane, grabbing for a roll of paper towels to mop her up. Ruby tore her eyes away from Melba and turned, with her mouth open, to Miss Mattie. Nothing came out. She was peppered with dust from crawling under the backstage curtain, and her red hair slopped out of its ponytail and stuck out in a dozen different directions.

Melba stood like a statue. Tot grabbed a drop cloth from the floor and wrapped it around Melba Jane. "She's in shock." She picked her up in her large arms, paint oozing everywhere. "Where's the bathroom? We need water."

Miss Mattie whirled away from Ruby. "The hose is out back. She needs to be hosed off now, if that paint's going to come off."

Tot shook her head. "She needs warmth." She looked at Melba. "Bless your heart. We'll fix you right up, sweetheart, bless your heart." Melba's eyes were closed. She looked dead.

Mrs. Varnado had recovered her wits. "This way." She led the way to the girls' bathroom. Ruby followed the crowd, trying to explain. "It was an accident…honest. I didn't mean for Bemmie to get in here. I was just keeping her away from Ivy...Ivy's about to have chicks, and..." Her voice trailed off as a low wailing began inside the girls' bathroom.

Ruby felt tears sting the corners of her eyes. She pushed her way outside. She left the wagon under the chinaberry tree and ran for the Pink Palace. Surely she would find Bemmie there. She wished Miss Eula would be there, too. She would listen to Ruby spill the whole story. Then she'd have all the right things to say to make her feel better. But she wasn't there. She'd have to find a way to feel better all by herself.

Dear Miss Eula,

I found Bemmie. She was safe in the Butterfields' chicken yard. She and Herman were squawking up a storm. Her feet are bright blue.

Melba's mama was in the middle of a permanent wave for Mrs. Popham but quit it to put Melba in the shower. Mama says she is still kind of blue, but she is all right, except her hair. Melba is telling everyone I did it on purpose.

I am sleeping with the chickens tonight, on our quilt. Dove was going to come but didn't. I don't care. I am going to watch Ivy's chicks come into the world. They are still peeping, and any minute they will crack out of their shells.

> Love,
> your (lonesome again) granddaughter,
> Ruby L.

Pee Ess: There is a full moon tonight. I have a lantern with batteries, a big flashlight, a canteen of water, two Moon Pies (lucky number), and the dictionary, so I can read calming words to Ivy while the chicks hatch. I wish you were here.

14

"Moreover...moron...morose..." Ruby had opened the dictionary on the counter, propped her elbows on either side of it, and read randomly on the page. She sat on a stool she'd dragged into the greenhouse. Her lantern glowed next to her head. She'd had leftover corn bread crumbled in buttermilk for supper, as her mother had spent so much time at the Lathams', she had come home late, and Ruby had said she wasn't hungry anyway.

"You and Melba need to talk," her mother had said, but Ruby had refused to go with her to the Lathams'.

Someone tapped on the greenhouse door. "It's me."

"Dove!" Ruby slid off the stool and opened the door. "Come in quick—Bemmie is out there, roosting with Bess. She wants like anything to get in here with Ivy and these new chicks."

"Are they here yet?" Dove had a sleeping bag in her arms and a backpack looped over her shoulders. She wore the same clothes she had worn ever since Ruby met her.

"Not yet. Boy, am I glad to see you!"

"Me, too." Dove rolled out her sleeping bag next to Ruby's quilt. They had just enough room.

"I thought you weren't coming. What happened today—it really was an accident."

"I know it was. I was just so…so…shocked! Everybody was. Miss Mattie was so mad at you, and she thought you did it on purpose, and I didn't know, because, how would I know? I already saw how you and Melba don't get along, and—"

Ruby tried to interrupt. "How can you talk like that, without taking a breath?"

"—and I met your mama, at the Lathams'. I like her. She told Aunt Tot and everybody else that you were trying to keep Bemmie away from Ivy, just like you said, and then she and Melba's mama talked in the corner for a while—I didn't get that on tape— and then Melba's mama patted your mama on the arm and went back to Melba, and Miss Mattie said, 'Evelyn, you've got to do something with that child,' and your mama said—I've got that part on tape! Do you want to hear it?"

"No." Ruby wanted to hear it more than anything.

"Well, never mind then. I brought my equipment with me tonight. I've got a fresh tape—let me label it."

Dove unzipped her backpack and pulled out her tape recorder and camera. She opened her notebook to a clean page, looked at her pocket watch, and wrote:

> June 26. Inside the chicken house at the Pink Palace, just outside the town of Halleluia, Mississippi, 10:07 p.m., waiting for Ruby Lavender's chicks to hatch. This will be recorded on tape 7, and here are <u>My Impressions</u> of this event, which I will record here, faithfully.
>
>   Signed,
>   Helen Dove Ishee,
>   Junior Anthropologist-in-Training

She picked up some clay pots and moved them to the shelf above her. Then she pushed buttons and made sure her tape was ready. After a few quiet minutes, she frowned and looked at Ruby. "Did you hear that Melba had to have her hair cut off?"

Ruby pulled her knees up to her chin but said nothing.

"She looks just awful."

Ruby crossed her arms on top of her knees and still was silent.

"Pitiful!" said Dove.

Ruby shot Dove her shut-up! look, but Dove didn't get it. "Do you want to hear my interview with her? I did it after she got her hair cut off. She'd just looked in the mirror. It's loud and you can hear every single word."

"I don't want to hear it," snapped Ruby.

She pulled up her overalls strap. "Mama already told me about Melba's hair, Dove."

Dove just looked at Ruby. Ruby fidgeted. "Okay," she admitted. "It looked awful when she was standing there with that paint dripping all over her." She pushed her hair out of her face. "But it wasn't my fault." She rested her forehead on her crossed arms and sighed through her knees. "I don't like Melba. And I hate it that you do."

A fly buzzed somewhere around Ruby's head. Outside, Bemmie and Bess began squawking. "They should be sleeping," said Ruby.

"Why don't you like her?"

"She hates me."

"Why does she hate you?"

Ruby used the palm of her hand to wipe the sweat from her upper lip. "No good reason."

"There must be some reason."

"She's a bully."

"She's been nice to me."

"Good for you. You're new here. She wants to know all about you right now. Just like everybody else."

Dove stretched out on her sleeping bag and began scribbling. Bemmie and Bess kept squawking, and Ruby stood up. "I need to check on the chickens. Maybe there's a skunk out there..."

Dove ignored her. "Peas, why is Melba so mad at you about the accident last summer? What happened last summer?"

15

Ruby changed the subject. "Why do you always wear the same clothes, Dove? Don't you have any others?" She made a shield with her hands and looked through the windowed walls of the greenhouse but saw nothing unusual in the moonlit chicken yard.

Dove was already in the middle of an explanation. "I've got lots. They are all the same. I had my mama buy me six shirts and six pants, all alike, and of course the socks come in a package of six, just alike, and then I always wear my hat and boots. I like these clothes. They're good for anthropology work; they're field clothes."

"Then they're uniforms, like the army, or a garage mechanic." Ruby's stomach growled, and she squatted under the counter to find her Moon Pies. "Did you eat tonight?"

Dove nodded. "That's why I was late. I ate with your aunt."

"Miss Mattie?"

"Yep. She had me and Aunt Tot and Uncle Tater over for dinner after Melba got cleaned up. What are you doing?"

Ruby shoved aside a bag of lime and searched under the counter. "I bet the whole town was at Melba's house."

"There was a reporter there, too. She was real old and wrinkly and powdery. Miss Mattie said she lives next door to Miss Eula and has no sense. She said, 'Don't talk to her, whatever you do,' so I didn't. But I took lots of notes. It's a stroke of luck to be ready with your equipment when there's a real-life tragedy, so you can get all the interviews firsthand, especially when people will talk and tell you all about it. I wanted to snap a picture of Melba to compare to the ones I took of her yesterday, but I didn't think she'd let me."

"It was just a bucket of paint!"

"Well, it's some powerful paint! Melba's head is stained bright blue in splotches like a patchwork.

Mr. Popham said, 'The only way to get that blue off of her noggin is to soak it in turpentine,' and then Melba started wailing again and her mama said, 'Harvey, you're not helping,' and she asked everybody to go home, but I talked to Melba for a few minutes in her room—that's when I tape-recorded her."

Ruby spied the Moon Pies but couldn't reach them. Her voice was muffled from under the counter. "Serves her right, after making fun of my chickens the way she did. Her hair was ugly anyway."

"At least she *had* some! She's so mad at you!"

Bess squawked louder and Ruby listened. Then Bess quieted. "What's the matter with those two?" Ruby pulled the Moon Pies closer, using a broom handle, then reached farther and clawed them to her. "Got 'em!" she cheered. "They're kind of smushed." She crawled backward from under the counter and threw herself on her quilt. "Who cares if Melba is mad at me? I don't. I don't care about her at all."

"Well, I do."

Ruby glared at Dove. "You just want to record your gossipy old stories—that's all you want to do. You're just as nosy as Miss Phoebe and her column."

Dove's face colored and she picked at some straw on her sock. Ruby sighed. "Sorry. Really." She handed

Dove a Moon Pie, keeping the most smushed one for herself, hoping Dove would notice. Dove took it but didn't say anything about getting the best one.

Ruby pushed her hair out of her face. "I didn't mean it. I know your...work...is important," she said.

Dove unwrapped her Moon Pie. "I'd hate to be bald..." was all she said. She took a bite of her pie, then, looking thoughtful, started talking with her mouth full. "I mean, monks in Tibet are bald; they plan it that way, and they all look the same. They even wear the same clothes—these old potato-sack robes—and they fold their arms just so and smile just so and look all peaceful all the time. I bet it's a rule they have to look peaceful all the time—I'll find out when I go there—and they're bald, but here...here only old men are bald and that looks fine. But kids' being bald, that looks weird, and being blue is even worse. I don't know anybody who is blue on purpose."

Ruby flopped herself backward. "For heaven's sake, Dove!"

Outside, the chickens gave another squawk. "Go to sleep, girls!" called Ruby.

Ivy began clucking in earnest and moving on the nest, a little left, a little right, then settling again.

Dove's eyes grew wide. "Hey! Is that peeping I hear?"

"Yes sirree!" crowed Ruby. She tossed her Moon Pie onto her quilt and leaned closer to Ivy. "Put your head close to the nest, and you can hear the chicks pecking on their shells."

"Good golly!" Dove's Moon Pie was smashed under her left knee. "How does it work? What happens next?"

"As long as the chicks are warm under Ivy and pecking on their shells, they are growing stronger. They'll peck a line all the way around the middle of the shell, and then they'll push hard with their feet and wiggle out. They have to do it themselves, or they won't be strong enough to live in the world. Ivy's clucks mean 'Come on, you can do it.'"

Dove listened. "They're talking to each other already."

Outside in the moonlit night, Bess and Bemmie began talking too, squawking loudly again. And this time they didn't stop.

"Hush up, you hens!" yelled Ruby. But Bemmie and Bess screeched longer and louder, and suddenly Ruby knew: Something was terribly wrong.

16

Dove blinked. "What's going on?" Ruby flung open the greenhouse door and pushed herself into the warm night air. She saw Bess racing through the chicken yard, panicked. Ruby's heart began a hard thump in her chest. She couldn't see Bemmie anywhere. She tore back into the greenhouse. "Throw me a rag from that bucket, Dove!" Now Ruby's heart raced, *hurry-hurry*.

Dove was on her feet. "What for?"

"I'll throw it over Bess's eyes so I can catch her. Hurry!"

Dove lunged for the bucket, kicking it and wedging it between bales of straw.

Thunk! Something heavy hit the ground beside the door where Ruby was waiting. Bess screamed. Ruby focused her eyes in the moonlit dark. Now she saw them—rocks littered the yard! Ruby kept the chicken yard clean and dirt-smooth—someone was throwing rocks! Ruby couldn't breathe. She held the greenhouse door open with her foot and stretched her arms out to Dove. "Hurry, Dove!"

Dove threw a handful of rags at Ruby. Ruby grabbed for them and stumbled.

Thonk! Again. Another rock. And *spap!* Again. Desperate, Ruby scrambled to her feet, bringing the rags with her, and reached for the door. But before she could get back outside, a shattering sound deafened her. Her hands flew to her ears and she screamed. Dove screamed. The girls ducked, covering their heads as a greenhouse window fell into a million crumbling pieces and glass showered them. The lantern fell and went out.

"Ruby!" Dove was under the counter, but Ruby was near the door. She lay still, in a ball, on her quilt. Moonlight streamed through the windows and across her back.

"Ruby!" Dove screamed. Slowly, Ruby lifted her head and took a breath. Yes, she was alive. "Are you okay?" Ruby nodded and spit. Glass was all around her, maybe even in her mouth, but she was okay. Dove was okay, Ivy was...

Ruby couldn't see the nest. "Where's Ivy!"

Dove jumped to her feet. "Her nest is turned over! I don't see her!"

Ruby panicked. She crawled under the counter, ignoring the glass as it scraped at her. Bess had slammed the greenhouse door shut, trying to get inside, and now she scrabbled against it, squawking to get in. Ruby didn't hear her; she called for Ivy. "Where are you, Ivy?" Dread washed over her. "Where's the lantern, Dove? Do you have the flashlight?" Ruby stretched out her hands and felt gingerly around the greenhouse floor in the shadow-darkness. Her right hand touched feathers, and a frightened chicken pecked her hand. "Ivy! Ouch! Here she is!"

Ruby's hand closed around the flashlight. She switched it on and played it over the floor of the greenhouse. There was Ivy, next to a bag of peat moss, sitting quietly on a pile of straw that had fallen out of the overturned peach basket. Beside Ivy was a large rock with a note attached by a rubber band.

"Oh-my-gosh, Ivy, oh-my-gosh."

"Here's an egg!" Dove sounded triumphant, then suddenly defeated. "It's broken to pieces." Her voice was full of cracks. "Here's another. Oh, no!..." Her voice trailed off.

Ruby didn't hear her. "She doesn't want me to touch her. I don't know if she's hurt."

"I can only find two eggs. Let me have the flashlight, Ruby." Dove took the flashlight from Ruby. "Here, help me look, we've got to find the other egg. These two are—"

Ruby rallied. "What? They're what?"

"Broken. Just broken. Broken to bits."

"Let me see," ordered Ruby. Her voice curdled in her throat. Dove played the flashlight on the eggs she had found. They lay cracked opened with warm, wet chicks inside. There was no movement or sound from them. They had dropped too far and cracked open too soon for the chicks to survive on their own.

Ruby was numb. She stared at her chicks.... They were here, peeping and pecking...and now they were not. "No!" she whispered it. She didn't hear anything—no peeping, no pecking.... *"No!"* she shouted. She sprang to her feet and barreled out the door. She looked for her chickens and saw bobbing lights and shadows dressed in bathrobes hurrying toward the Pink Palace. Bess was roosting and looked unhurt.

Ruby couldn't think. She walked back inside and lowered herself onto a straw bale, using her hands for balance. Her voice crumbled. "I don't know where Bemmie is. People are coming. I don't want them here."

"We need help, Ruby. Look at us!"

By the moon's light, Ruby could see that her hands were bleeding. Dove had a long scratch on her forehead. The broken eggs lay still, their almost-born chicks inside. Ruby touched them tenderly. A lump started in her throat, hard and huge. She felt the sting of tears at her eyes.

"Ivy's sitting on the third egg, Ruby. It's still peeping." In the silence, Ruby could hear a faint peeping coming from under Ivy. Ivy clucked back. She would not move from her egg.

Ruby heard her mother's voice, full of concern, and Miss Mattie's, in charge. One tear spilled down Ruby's cheek. She gritted her teeth and willed it away. She picked up the rock that had come through the glass, removed the rubber band, and opened the note. It said:

I hate you, Ruby Lavender,
and I hate your stupid chickens.

It wasn't signed. It didn't need signing; Ruby knew who had done this. Soon, everyone would know. Ruby crumpled the note and waited for the door of the greenhouse to open.

17

The questions came.

"What in the world?"

"Are you girls all right?"

"Watch where you're stepping, folks!"

Somebody had found the lantern and turned it on. Flashlights played around the greenhouse, making spotlights in the lantern glow. Ruby's mother crouched in front of the girls and looked them over carefully.

"We're all scratched up." Dove's voice choked in her throat.

"Ruby honey?" Her mother placed her hand on Ruby's back.

Miss Mattie stood in the doorway. "They're scared half to death, Evelyn, but they're fine."

Ruby's mother frowned. "I don't know…"

Ruby was doubled over with her head on her knees. Her fists clenched the note, and she was breathing hard. Dove began to cry.

Now Miss Mattie was examining the damage. "Most of these panes are safety glass. It could have been worse. They're lucky."

"Lucky!" Ruby lifted her head. A dust streak swam down her cheek. "Look at Ivy! Look at the chicks! I know who did this—it's Melba Jane! She killed Ivy's chicks."

Ruby's anger pulled her together. She shuddered all over and pointed at the eggs on the ground. Her mother stooped under the counter and looked. The chicks still did not move.

Miss Mattie put a hand lightly over her mouth, then fished in her pocket and pulled out a handkerchief. She handed it to Ruby's mother. "I can't imagine she meant to do this, but you're right, she probably did. I saw her running away from here like a scared jackrabbit."

"I know she did it! Here's her note! It's her!" Ruby brandished the crumpled note and waved it in front of Miss Mattie, but she wouldn't give it up.

"Where's the third egg, sweetie?" Ruby's mother dabbed at a dribble of blood that made its way down the back of Ruby's hand. She looked like she might cry herself.

Dove sniffed. "Ivy's sitting on it. It's still peeping."

Miss Mattie left the doorway. Ruby heard her talking to Mr. Harvey Popham outside. "Go on over to the Lathams' and get Leila and Melba Jane..."

"Don't you bring her here!" Ruby leaped to her feet. "Don't you bring her anywhere near my chickens! Bemmie is missing, too. I don't know where she went. Melba left the gate open."

Ruby wiped her hair from her face and left a streak of blood on her cheek.

"You're bleeding, honey." Her mother stood and held Ruby's face in her hands. She looked intently into Ruby's eyes. "First things first. Let's take care of these cuts and scrapes—you, too, Dove. Come on into the house, where we can see."

"I'm not leaving my chickens." Ruby wiped her nose on her shirtsleeve.

Miss Mattie used her in-charge voice. "Ruby, you come with me, now. You, too, Dove. We're going to clean you up. Evelyn, can you manage here?"

"Yes, ma'am." Ruby's mother sounded relieved.

"I won't go!" Ruby stared at her mother.

Miss Mattie held out her hand. "I'll bring you

back directly. You won't be any good to these chickens if you get tetanus. Now let's get cleaned up and make sure you aren't carrying glass in those cuts."

Ruby's mother nodded. "I'm going to take care of this glass with Mr. Harvey. When you come back, we'll be able to think more clearly, okay?"

Ruby faced Miss Mattie. "You're not bringing Melba Jane here, are you?"

"No, I won't do that. We've got other things to attend to right now."

Ruby smelled the dirt of the chicken yard and the straw from Ivy's nest. Ivy clucked from her perch on top of the last egg. "I'll be right back, Ivy girl. You are such a brave chicken." She turned to her mother. "Look at how she tried to protect her chicks." Her voice choked again, and tears were fresh in her eyes.

Her mother's eyes filled with tears, too. She hugged Ruby. "You've done what you could do, honey." She put an arm around the sniffling Dove. "I'm going to call your aunt and uncle and tell them what happened. I'll tell them you're okay. All right?"

Dove nodded. She sniffed again and wiped her nose with the back of her hand. Then she followed Ruby out of the greenhouse. She walked onto the porch of the Pink Palace with Ruby and Miss Mattie. The three of them disappeared into the house.

18

Soap and water stung Ruby's skin, but Miss Mattie's no-nonsense way was a comfort. She helped wash each girl's hair carefully in the big kitchen sink. Then she had each one take a shower in Miss Eula's pink bathroom. She found Hawaiian muumuus, sent by Johnson, on the back of Miss Eula's bedroom door and had the girls wear them while she fixed cuts and scrapes.

"It's a wonder you two weren't cut worse than this," she mused, as she finished dabbing both girls with Mercurochrome.

"I was under the counter," said Dove. She was still pale.

"Thank goodness for small favors."

Ruby had been silent all through her head wash, through her shower. She had had no comment when

Miss Mattie found six pink muumuus behind Miss Eula's door and rolled her eyes and shook her head. She sat in the kitchen at Miss Eula's table, closed her eyes, and took a deep breath. If she tried, she could smell her grandmother. She could even smell her grandfather and imagine he was in the room, in his overalls, getting ready to pot geraniums in his green-house. She missed them both so much.

"Do you hear from Miss Eula, Miss Mattie?"

Miss Mattie looked up from her dabbing. "I do." She sounded tired. Ruby wondered what time it was.

"Does she ever say when she's coming back?"

"No, she doesn't." Miss Mattie put the cotton balls back where she had found them, in a bread box labeled FIRST AID. HELP! HELP!

"Do you miss her?"

"I expect I do."

Ruby felt the hard lump in her throat again. "You do? Really?"

"Well, of course I do, child. She's my sister-in-law."

Dove walked out to the back porch in her muu-muu, a towel wrapped around her head. Miss Mattie sat down in a kitchen chair. "What's this about?"

Ruby blinked at Miss Mattie. "I don't know. I just wondered." She hesitated, then spoke. "I don't know what to do now. I wish Miss Eula was here and she could tell me. I don't know where Bemmie is—she could be lying in a ditch somewhere."

"Oh, now, you know better than that. That blue-footed floozy is off to the Butterfields' the minute that gate is opened. I bet she's there right now, helping herself to the corn and chatting with Herman."

"I need to go find her."

"Wait for morning, honey. It'll keep until morning. Bemmie is a resourceful old girl."

"So what do I do now?"

"Right now all we can do is take care of what's in front of us."

Ruby sniffed. "I want to have a funeral."

"For the chicks?"

Ruby's lower lip quivered. "Yes, just like the one we had for Grandpa Garnet. Will you come?"

Miss Mattie sighed. "Yes. I will come, Ruby." She touched Ruby's wet hair. "Let me comb this out for you now." Ruby didn't protest, and Miss Mattie pulled a comb from her pocket and began, gently, to comb Ruby's hair. "When you lose someone you love, it hurts, doesn't it?"

Ruby nodded slowly. A fat tear dropped off the end of her nose. She sniffed loudly. "I'm a crybaby."

"Oh, honey, we've all dampened a pillow in our

day. There's no shame in crying." She handed Ruby a tissue.

Ruby blew her nose. "Well, I don't cry anymore."

"Why ever not?" Miss Mattie worked on a tangle in Ruby's hair.

"Last summer, when Grandpa Garnet died, Melba Jane laughed at me for crying at his funeral. She said I was no better than a baby and she would tell everybody in school that I was a selfish coward besides."

"Well, Melba said plenty of things she shouldn't have said last summer, Ruby. And you can bet she cried plenty. I know her mama did. My goodness, so did I."

Ruby sat still while Miss Mattie glided her comb smoothly through Ruby's long red hair. Ruby sniffed. "I'm sorry about ruining the operetta this year."

"You didn't ruin it, child. The operetta will be fine, one way or another. There's always another day. Matter of fact, I think this day is about to dawn."

Miss Mattie took an elastic out of her pocket and pulled Ruby's hair into a neat ponytail. "There. I hardly recognize you. But I like it."

Ruby looked Miss Mattie in the eye. "Miss Mattie?"

"Hmmmm?"

"Do you ever laugh?"

"No. Never." Miss Mattie smiled a smile that softened her whole face. It surprised Ruby so much, she smiled back.

"Good." Miss Mattie gave Ruby's shoulder a pat. "You're going to be all right. Don't worry. This family is full of strong women who know how to laugh."

Ruby nodded and blew her nose again.

"Ruby!" It was Dove, calling in a voice full of excitement.

"What in the world?..." Miss Mattie opened the back door.

"Ruby! Ruby, come quick! The new chick is coming—*now!*"

19

Miss Mattie made coffee in Miss Eula's kitchen, and Ruby's mother joined her. The neighbors made their way home. In the greenhouse, the broken glass was gone. Ruby's mother had placed the cracked eggs in a small basket on the counter and covered them with a cloth napkin from the kitchen. She had put some of Grandpa Garnet's black-eyed Susans in a Mason jar of water and put them next to the basket. Now Ruby and Dove leaned against a straw bale in the greenhouse, wearing Miss Eula's muumuus, watching.

Ivy clucked loudly, encouraging her chick. The moon lit the greenhouse with a silver glow, and the air smelled like straw and morning dew.

Ruby got on her hands and knees and peered

closely under Ivy. "She's out! She's out, but she's staying under Ivy to keep warm and to dry her feathers."

The girls waited, and the summer sky lightened. Dove spread her fingers and smoothed her muumuu with the palms of her hands. "Are you okay?"

Ruby nodded. "I'm okay. Are you?"

"I was so scared."

"Me, too." Ruby eyed Dove. "You look different when you're not wearing your uniform."

"So do you. I never see you in anything but your overalls." Dove stifled a yawn. "What are you going to do now?"

"I don't know. I'll write Miss Eula. She'll know what to do."

"What will she say?"

"I was thinking about it. When something terrible happens, Miss Eula says, 'Life does go on,' but it doesn't, does it? Those chicks will never have a life now."

Dove thought about it. "I don't know. Maybe it means something else." She took the towel off her head and used it to rub her hair vigorously. Ruby was surprised to see the short white tips stand in place, just like they always did.

Ivy squawked, stood up, ruffled her feathers, stepped off the straw...and there she was, Ivy's chick. She was still damp, but her feathers were drying. She was cornmeal yellow, tiny and new. She shook herself, like a puppy, and peeped three times. She tried to take a step and stumbled. Ivy stepped back over her and covered her chick. She clucked. The chick peeped. Mother and child settled themselves again.

"Good golly!" Dove held her hands under her chin. "Oh my golly."

Ruby's heart pounded in a smooth, hard rhythm, *she's here! she's here!* Ivy's chick was here. Ruby was sure the chick had seen her, knew her. After all, she'd heard Ruby's voice for weeks. Ruby thought about the day she and Miss Eula had rescued Ivy and Bemmie and Bess. It was a lifetime ago. Since then, Ivy had laid three eggs. Miss Eula had left. Dove had come. And Melba had ruined everything. Almost everything. Ruby didn't know what to do about that, and she was too heartsick to think.

Bone tired, thought Ruby, *I'm bone tired.* The stars were winking out overhead. The first morning birds welcomed a new day. Ruby pressed her fingers to her lips and kissed them, then turned them out, toward Ivy. That was for the new chick. She blinked, stood up to stretch, and looked silently at the small basket on the counter. She brushed her fingertips across the petals of the black-eyed Susans. She swallowed back her tears. "It'll be a long time before Ivy gets off the nest and lets her chick walk around. We should go to sleep."

"Good." Dove rubbed her eyes with the heels of her hands. "I'm so tired I can hardly stand it."

"It'll be too hot out here soon—let's go in. Miss Eula won't mind if we sleep in her bed."

Ruby's mother tucked the girls in. She kissed them both on their foreheads and then on their eyelids. "Sleep tight. I'm walking over to the Butterfields' to get Bemmie—they called a little while ago and they've got her. Then Miss Mattie and I are going to the Lathams'. Dove, your aunt and uncle are coming to check on you in a few hours. Your aunt said she was making you breakfast. You girls get some sleep. When that new chick is ready, we all want to welcome her into the world." She smiled and touched Ruby's cheek.

Miss Eula's bed was enormous. The girls had three pink pillows apiece. They lay under a pink sheet, wearing pink muumuus, with their eyes closed for a long time, listening to the birds through the screened windows. *Peaceful,* thought Ruby. It was peaceful. Dove's tape recorder and camera lay on the dresser. She hadn't taken a single picture, hadn't recorded a sound.

"I hear the sunflowers growing outside the window," Ruby said.

"Can you really hear them growing?"

"My grandpa always said you could hear all living things if you listened. He used to talk to his flowers, especially the black-eyed Susans. He called them 'the Girls.' He said, 'They all look alike, and they're all named Susan.' And then he'd laugh."

"I like that," said Dove.

"Me, too."

The girls were silent for a moment, listening. Then Dove turned over and faced the wall. "Peas?"

"Yeah?"

"I'm glad you're my friend." Dove sounded sleepy. She pulled up the sheet and tucked it under her chin.

Ruby turned onto her side and faced the window. "What am I going to do now, Dove?"

"I don't know, Peas." Dove's voice was drowsy and soft.

"What would *you* do?"

Dove didn't answer. Her breath was smooth and rhythmic, in and out. Ruby lay there a long time, listening to Dove sleep, listening to the quiet. By and by, her eyes closed and she fell deeply asleep and dreamed of her grandpa Garnet. He was kneeling in his garden, digging for worms with a silver trowel. Three soft yellow chicks cheeped around his knees. He talked to them and called them "the Girls." Ruby walked toward him and he waved at her and told her he was home now and she should get ready; he was taking her fishing on an early August morning. Taking her on a fishing trip he had promised her all summer.

Aurora County News

Twilight Edition, June 27

Happenings in Halleluia
(Special Midweek Installment)

by Phoebe "Scoop" Tolbert

Just as this reporter settled down last
night to a bowl of mint ice cream and a re-
run of "Angel in My Pocket," what should
come out of the night but crashes and
screams!

Mr. Tolbert and I rushed up the street to
Miss Eula Dapplevine's abode, from whence
the screams came, and found a disturbing
scene: glass broken around the greenhouse, definitely a destructive act in
our quiet town, and two distraught girls,
Ruby Lavender and—visiting for the summer—Miss Helen Dove Ishee, niece of Halleluia School's new fourth-grade teacher,
Ferrell Ishee.

As it turns out, this fiasco comes on the heels of another equally disturbing incident, in which Melba Jane Latham, daughter of Leila and the late Lionel Latham, was doused with a can of peacock-blue paint after being scared out of her wits by a chicken owned by Ruby Lavender.

It is believed by all that both incidents were accidents at heart. The upshot is twofold: (1) that there has been death and destruction at the Pink Palace, as two chicks in the greenhouse died from falling out of the nest before hatching as a result of alleged rock throwing by Melba Jane Latham in retaliation for (2) the death of Melba Jane's acting career due to having her hair cut off at the roots, because of its irreversible blueness.

I am awaiting further developments and will have a write-up as soon as I know more.

Dear Miss Eula,

The funeral for the chicks was today. Dove came and so did Aunt Tot and Mr. Ishee and Mama and even Miss Mattie. She brought a bucket of zinnias from her garden and we sang "In the Sweet By and By." The chicks are buried near the elm tree. Mr. Ishee is making a marker for me. He is putting "To bloom in heaven" on it. I asked for that.

Melba told Mama she didn't mean to throw the rock through the window, just to throw it in the chicken yard, but she missed. Well, what did she expect? She can't throw a softball. She can't cast a fishing line. She can't climb a tree. She made apologies to Mama because I won't let her talk to me.

Mama says I can't have her arrested. Old Ezra Jackson gave Melba a job so she can pay for the window, and now she has to help clean out cow stalls and put down fresh straw. Ha! Miss I-don't-get-my-hands-dirty has her hands around pitch-forks stuck in you-know-what! She won't last one day.

For your information, Ivy is fine. I have

named the new chick Rosebud. I carry her with me everywhere, in my front overalls pocket. She sleeps in a box by my bed. Ivy said it was all right. When Rosebud peeps, I reach down and pat her. I do not have any free advice. I miss you. It feels like a year since you left.

> Love,
> your (weary) granddaughter,
> Ruby L.

Dear Miss Land of Paradise,

Miss Mattie convinced Melba Jane to stay in the operetta. She asked me to stay, too, but I said no. I will not be anywhere near Melba.

I heard Miss Mattie talking to Melba's mama in the store, and I bet it was about me and Melba. She said, "They'll work it out, Leila." Ha! That's what she thinks.

Dove is coming in a few minutes to play with Rosebud. For your information, we are going to have a picnic on your back porch. We do that a lot.

Free advice: A remembrance is better when there are lots of people around to remember. You should come home. I'll wait for you, and we can picnic in the cemetery when you come back.

> Love,
> your (new mother) granddaughter,
> Ruby L.

Pee Ess: I love the photographs you sent of Hortense. She's kind of cute, isn't she? Have you told her all about me?

Dear Ruby (very dear),

Sugar, I am so so sorry to hear about Ivy's chicks. When I read your letter, my heart sank right into my toes. Thank goodness for Miss Mattie, and your mama, and our good neighbors. (And I have heard about this from every one of them—it's amazing how tragedy brings out a desire to write long letters.)

There's just nothing that can make us feel better when someone we love dies, is there? I'm so glad you have Rosebud. I can't wait to meet her.

The funeral sounds lovely, and you sang one of Grandpa Garnet's favorite hymns. His other favorite was "Stop This Preaching, Before I Fall Asleep." Let me know if you do decide to do a remembrance. Maybe you could put a pillow on the pew where he always sat in church.

But don't worry about that now. Right now is for remembering those chicks and taking care of Rosebud. Take care of yourself, too. And Dove. You are brave girls, and I love you.

> Love,
> your (full of compassion) grandmother,
> Miss Eula

July 7

Dear Miss Grandmother of Two,

Melba sent me an "I'm sorry" note yesterday, but I tore it up. Sorry isn't good enough. Nothing is good enough.

Chickens grow fast. Rosebud outgrew her box already, and she doesn't fit in my pocket anymore, either. She follows me everywhere, like a little shadow. She waits outside Miss Mattie's store while I sweep.

Yesterday I told Miss Mattie she really wasn't such a crab. She said, "Whoever said that I was?" and I said, "Why...I don't know, Miss Mattie, but I know I heard it somewhere..."

Love,
your (thoughtful) granddaughter,
Ruby L.

Pee Ess: Dove has been wearing your muumuus. You sure have a lot of them. I hope you don't mind. She doesn't match as well as she used to, but she is excited about wearing "Polynesian outfits." She wears a muumuu and that hard brown hat and those boots and white socks. She wants to interview you when you come home.

Dear Ruby,

   I'm glad you think Leilani is cute—she is! And you are beautiful. Of COURSE I've told her all about you! She said, "I can't wait to meet my fabulous cousin." Well, she said, "Thhhwwaaaaagh!" but that's what she meant.

   You know, I have been thinking. I am wondering how you are going to avoid Melba Jane when school starts. Or when you are 10. Or when you are 25. Or when you are my age! That's a long time to never see somebody. Lots can happen in 50 or 60 years…or in a day. At least go to the operetta for me, won't you? I need someone reliable to give me a good review. I hate that I'm going to miss it.

   And don't worry about a remembrance for your grandpa; it was just a thought. There's a right time for everything, and when the time is right— if ever it is—you'll know it.

                     Love,
                     your (a bit homesick) grandmother,
                     Miss Eula

Dear Miss You Are Missing It,

Good garden of peas! Bemmie has laid an egg!!! I'm not kidding!

She and Herman have been sneaking out to meet each other at night. They are having what Miss Mattie calls "a clandestine romance." What's that? We should have a chick on August 1! Or maybe August 2. Either day is lucky, right? Bemmie squawks all the time. She is LOUD and proud of herself! Bess is such a lazybones, she just eats through all the noise, and even eats some for Bemmie. Ivy says she's happy for Bemmie and can give her some pointers.

For your information, I played catch with Cleebo Wilson yesterday. He had a bat, so we hit some pop flies to each other. He's a good batter. I'm a better catcher.

> Love,
> your (going to be a mother again)
> granddaughter,
> Ruby L.

Pee Ess: Mama is cooking with Dove's aunt Tot. She says it is exhausting.

Dear Ruby,

Of course Dove can wear my muumuus!—tell her it's my pleasure—just don't let her out in any high winds—she might get picked up and carried off, like a kite.

Now I'm about to have my picture taken with a bunch of bananas on Johnson's porch—a HUGE bunch of bananas. I bet there's a hundred bananas in this bunch. It's almost as tall as I am! I am going to sing "Yes, We Have No Bananas" when the shutter clicks.

Love,
your (missing you) grandmother,
Miss Eula

Dear Miss Banana Split,

Today I visited Aunt Tot and Mr. Ishee. Aunt Tot was painting on her porch. She paints the ugliest pictures in the world. Mr. Ishee tells her they are, "Lovely, darling Tot!" and Aunt Tot says, "What would I do without you, Tater?" and he kisses her and says, "I hope we never have to find out."

You must miss Grandpa Garnet worse than anybody.

For your information, Aunt Tot wants to hang the painting she did today in the new baby's room. "Wonderful idea, Tot!" said Mr. Ishee. I think he needs glasses.

Dove and I are wallpapering the baby's room. Aunt Tot has lots of choices papered to the wall already, and she can't make up her mind, so we are supposed to put all of them up, here and there. You would like Aunt Tot.

I miss you worse than anybody.

> Love,
>
> your (sticky) granddaughter,
> Ruby L.

Dear Ruby,

I am flabbergasted! I am stupefied with joy!
Bemmie has laid an EGG?? Oh joy and happy day!
How lovely that Bemmie and Herman are sweet on
each other—Bemmie is a woman after my own
heart. (Of course, Herman seems to be sweet on
just about anybody. Somebody's going to have to
talk to that man. He has no decorum.)

> Love,
> your (so happy I could go surfing—I think
> I will!) grandmother,
> Miss Eula

Dear Miss Lots Can Happen in 60 Years,

I just got your letter about Melba Jane.
Miss Eula, I don't want to see Melba. I don't
want to go to the operetta. I don't want to
do a remembrance for Grandpa Garnet.
You don't know what it's like. You live
there now, and I live here, and I know
what it's like.

I don't have waterfalls and hula dancing
and big bananas. I don't have Grandpa
Garnet, and I don't have you. But I have
the chickens and I have Mama and I have
Dove and I even have Miss Mattie and Mr.
Ishee and Aunt Tot and Miss Phoebe and
Mr. Harvey and whole bunches of other
people in Halleluia. And I don't have to
have Melba if I don't want to. So I don't.

I want you to come home. If you don't
want to, you don't have to. But that's what
I want. You said you wanted to live away
from reminders of Grandpa Garnet for a
while. I live with them every day, and I'm
all right.

Love,
your (a lot happens in a day and you
don't see it) granddaughter,
Ruby L.

20

August 1

I miss you at the schoolhouse." Dove bit into a mayonnaise sandwich and washed it down with root beer. She sat on the back-porch step, wearing a fuchsia muumuu and her brown boots.

"You've got Melba." Ruby lay in the porch swing, swinging herself by sticking one bare foot on the porch and pushing off sideways whenever she slowed to a stop. "I might melt, it's so hot."

Ivy, Bess, and Rosebud scratched the dirt in the chicken yard, looking for bugs. Bemmie nested and cackled from inside the greenhouse. The broken window was open to the sky. Ruby's mother had put a screen in the window frame.

Dove's mind was on the operetta. "You should come tonight and watch. Everybody's coming! It's going to be good. Melba has a solo."

Ruby rolled her eyes. "I bet you've filled up ten of those astropology tapes listening to her yap."

"Anthropology." Dove drank the last of her root beer. "She talks about her daddy a lot."

Ruby sat up. "What does she tell you?"

"She tells stories. She told a story about how he used to take her out all by herself, just the two of them, to stargaze in the summers. He taught her all the constellations. She can spot Orion's belt, and Scorpio's tail and the twins..."

A tiny shiver skittered up Ruby's spine. She closed her eyes and pulled a vision of Grandpa Garnet to mind, their firefly poem, and their nights with Miss Eula in the back meadow, under the stars.

"She showed me where the car went off the bridge."

Ruby's eyes flew open. "She did? Well, I *never* go there."

"Is that why you always take the long way to town?"

Ruby pushed off with her toes and the swing began its back-and-forth again. "Yes," she said, quietly. "That's why I go the long way." She stared at a mud-dauber nest on the porch ceiling, and as she tried not to think about them, memories of last summer began to lay on her like a blanket of hot air. She covered her face with her hands and breathed between her fingers. She saw her grandfather, standing on the Lake Jasper bridge, waving to her. She rubbed her face and shook her head to clear it, and saw Dove looking at her. She gave a little laugh. "I don't even know where the car went off the bridge."

Dove spoke carefully. "I can show you."

Ruby studied the hair on her arms. "I don't want to know."

There was silence then, except for the cackles from the greenhouse. Ruby watched her chickens. She looked at the mass of black-eyed Susans growing next to the chicken-yard gate. Miss Eula's words came to her, floating on the breeze and pushing the hot air away. *Just a remembrance to mark the fact that Garnet was in this world, and that the world was a good place because he was here.*

"Maybe I do want to know," Ruby murmured.

Dove stood and brushed sandwich crumbs off the front of her muumuu. "Come on, then."

Ruby looked at her bare feet. She spread her toes out as far as they would go. They looked like little fans.

"I'll go with you," said Dove.

Ruby's eyes met Dove's. She gave a determined boost and pushed herself off the swing. The chain jingled. She took two hats from the hat pegs by the door and gave one to Dove. "Just a minute," she said. "There's something I need." She went inside the Pink Palace and came back with some scissors. She clipped a bunch of black-eyed Susans and tied them with a piece of twine from her pocket. Then she said to Dove, "Okay. Let's go."

"Who are the flowers for?"

"They're for me," said Ruby.

The girls set off, turning left onto the road toward town.

21

The cicadas shrilled from the trees. "It's too hot to spit," said Ruby. She spit anyway.

"It sure is a lot shorter to town this way than the way you go," said Dove. Orange dust kicked up on the road where the girls walked, past fat goldenrod blooming like feathery yellow clouds. They reached the end of the road and saw the bridge on their right, across the paved road that turned into Main Street and town. Ruby stood a long time, looking at it.

"My grandpa Garnet never got to this side of the bridge." Her voice was flat, without feeling. Her stomach hurt. She pushed her hair out of her face. If Melba could come to this bridge, so could she. So could she. It was a wooden bridge that clattered whenever a car crossed it, and there were roomy walkways on either side, made just for people traffic, or bicycle traffic, or—as Grandpa Garnet used to say—for dog, raccoon, and fox traffic. Soon Ruby was standing with Dove on the Lake Jasper bridge in the middle of the afternoon. The sun was almost straight overhead. It blinked on and off through the clouds, shining on the bridgework.

"Right there." Dove pointed to a spot almost halfway across the bridge. Ruby could see where it had been repaired. She walked to the railing and touched the spot. She made herself look down into the lake. Ruby had been swimming in it a thousand times. The water had felt so good on her skin. But she would never, *never* swim in Lake Jasper again. Her fist was hot and sweaty where she held the black-eyed Susans. She stuck them in the side pocket of her overalls, where they stuck out like a black-and-yellow flag.

A feeling of weariness took over, and Ruby leaned against the bridge, her stomach folding into itself along the rail. She looked at her wavy reflection in the water below. "It was my fault," she said. A tingle started in her chest and spread to her throat.

"What was?"

"The accident."

Dove frowned. "Why do you say that?"

Ruby took a deep breath and let it out. "Sheriff

Varnado said Grandpa Garnet fell asleep at the wheel. That's all they could figure. But I know more, and so does Melba."

Dove's face colored. "What happened?" A tractor rumbled over the bridge. The driver waved at them.

Ruby kept going. "Remember how, the day we had root-beer floats at your house, Melba said that my grandpa and her daddy were supposed to stay in Raleigh, but they didn't?"

Dove nodded.

"It was *my* fault, because they were going to stay over in Raleigh that night, but I didn't want them to; I wanted Grandpa Garnet to come home because he had promised me a special fishing day—just him and me—and I had begged him to come back so we could go early and have a whole entire day, from sunup to sundown, breakfast, dinner, and supper. We were standing by the car, just me and Melba and her daddy and my grandpa, and Melba heard me asking Grandpa Garnet to please, please, please come back that night. And Melba's daddy was saying, 'I don't know. It's a long drive late at night, Ruby. I expect we'll stay over,' and Grandpa Garnet was saying, 'Don't you worry about a thing, Ruby. We'll have our day,' and we didn't. And if he had stayed in Raleigh, we would have had it, we would have had our day!

Now I don't have a grandpa, Melba doesn't have a daddy, we don't have any days left!"

Ruby wrapped her arms around herself and held her elbows. She didn't want to cry. Her head hurt. She closed her eyes and listened to a catbird call from somewhere in the trees.

Dove took off her hat and ran her fingers through her white hair. She leaned against the bridge with her elbows on the railing. "Ruby…"

Ruby's voice choked. "Melba holds it over me; she knows I'm afraid she'll tell everybody. And maybe she did—maybe they know it already! Maybe they all think it was my fault."

"Ruby, that's not right—"

Ruby barreled ahead. "Melba told me that her daddy always stayed over when the Grange met in Raleigh, and my grandpa would have stayed for him, if I hadn't asked him to come home." Her heart hurt, it cramped in her chest, and she squeezed her eyes shut.

Grasshoppers called from the tall grass, and another car rattled over the bridge. Ruby dropped her head and gave Dove a weary smile. "Too bad you don't have your equipment with you now, huh?" Dove blinked and Ruby explained. "Here's a firsthand interview, Dove. Here's a tragedy. Here's the whole story."

It took Dove only a moment to find her voice. "There's some things you don't report on. I bet Margaret Mead didn't tape everything. Some things are...personal."

Ruby rested her elbows on the bridge railing next to Dove and put her face into her hands for a long minute. Dove turned around to face the opposite side of the bridge. She scratched the side of her face.

"I know something you don't," she said.

"What?" Ruby spoke from inside her hands.

Dove thought for a minute, then spoke. "Remember when I told you that I met Miss Mattie at the mercantile and she told Aunt Tot and me all about the accident?"

"Ummmm."

"Aunt Tot asked Miss Mattie why ever didn't your grandpa and Melba's daddy stay in Raleigh like they were supposed to. Miss Mattie stopped mixing the paint and said she knew her brother and that he had never for a minute entertained the notion of staying in Raleigh overnight, that he had never spent a night away from Miss Eula and he wasn't about to start that night."

Ruby lifted her face out of her hands and stared at Dove.

Dove knit her eyebrows together with a pained look. "I thought you knew that!"

Ruby opened her mouth, then shut it.

Dove scratched her head. "Well, I did. I just thought you knew...I mean, if I knew you thought it was your fault and I knew it wasn't, I would have told you lots earlier, but I didn't know it. I never for a minute thought it was your fault, and I didn't think you thought it was your fault..." Dove's voice trailed off, and she cocked her head and peered at Ruby.

Ruby frowned. "I didn't know that...," she said in a soft voice. Her pulse began a *ping-ping-ping* sound in her ears and her heart beat faster. "Or maybe I did and I forgot. I don't know if that's true or not." She pushed her hair away from her face with both hands. Then slowly a new thought crept into Ruby's head. She looked at Dove with earnest eyes. She could hardly get her breath. "Miss Mattie says she knows, but she doesn't. She doesn't know what Grandpa Garnet was thinking!"

Ruby began pacing on the bridge, back and forth, back and forth. "That's what Miss Mattie believes, but she doesn't know—nobody knows—why he decided what he did..." She stopped pacing and willed her heart to quiet itself. She felt dizzy. She gazed at a spot in the distance, not seeing anything. "I don't know what he was thinking…"

Dove's eyes lit up. "Or what Melba's daddy was thinking."

Ruby grabbed tight to this new thought. She knit her hands together and then pulled them apart. She knew something important. "Thing is," she said, lifting her head and breathing in the sweet smell of discovery, "thing is, Grandpa Garnet would have come home anyway. He always came home, always." A lightness slipped into Ruby's voice and a tingle ran from her shoulders right down to her toes. "He would have come home…no matter what."

Dove smiled.

Ruby's tingles turned into pinpricks of amazement. She tried to take it in, this new knowledge. She studied a spiderweb on the bridgework. It shimmered in the sunshine.

"I'll ask Miss Eula about it," said Ruby. "But I bet that's right. He would have come home." She watched a pair of dragonflies dancing on the water. She almost felt like dancing herself.

Dove tapped her hat back onto her head. "I've got to go soon. We're supposed to show up early so we have time to put on costumes and makeup and figure out what to do with Aunt Tot's…scenery. But I can stay a little bit longer if you want."

Ruby's heart felt light; it fluttered. "Go. You'll make Miss Mattie crazy if you're late."

"Come with me. It'll be fun."

Ruby shook her head. "I don't want to. I'll sit with Bemmie. Plus, I'm closing up for Miss Mattie at the mercantile. She forgets to turn out the lights and lock up on operetta night."

Dove took two steps toward the road and then stopped. "Can I sit up with you after the operetta and wait for Bemmie's egg to hatch?"

Ruby nodded. "Come over when you're done. Bring your equipment."

"Okay."

Ruby pulled on her earlobe. "Maybe I'll give you an interview."

Dove raised her eyebrows and Ruby shrugged. She shoved her hair out of her face.

"You know what, Dove?"

"What?"

"You're a good friend."

Dove squinted into the late-afternoon sun. "Yes," she said thoughtfully. "I *am*."

Dove walked away and Ruby lingered, waving to the few cars that came rattling across the bridge.

Soon she realized she didn't know how to leave. She didn't know what to do with her flowers. She should say something. She looked into the lake again. "You would have come home. You always came home." She untied the twine around her flowers. One by one, she tossed black-eyed Susans onto the lake. With each flower she remembered one good thing about her grandfather. "Good-bye, Grandpa Garnet," she whispered. "Good-bye."

She felt the tears coming, but she stopped them by gritting her teeth until her jaws hurt. She picked up her floppy hat and put it back on her head. She heard footsteps behind her, coming onto the bridge, coming toward her. Dove coming back to check on her. Dove wanting to make sure it was okay that she'd left her friend at the bridge.

Ruby hitched up her left overalls strap and turned. "I'm fine," she said, and almost choked on the words. It wasn't Dove standing in front of her. It was Melba Jane.

22

Ruby's legs felt like jelly under her. They wobbled, and she sat down hard, her back against the bridge railing. Melba stood there, a puzzled look on her face, as if trying to make up her mind, then she sat down next to Ruby. She was wearing a long brown wig, an enormous black hat, and purple gloves. When she sat down, her sundress covered her legs, knees to ankles. Her toes peeked out from under it, from where they were nestled in delicate white sandals. Ruby raised a dusty big toe and tried to think about what to do next. Get up? Run away? Spit on Melba? Nothing seemed quite right. Her hands shook in her lap. She opened them wide and clutched her knee-caps. The lake made a lapping sound below them, where the water met the shore.

Melba broke the silence. "I wanted to talk to

you…" She smoothed her dress down her legs to her ankles.

Ruby's head throbbed. She squeezed her knees with her hands.

Melba sucked in a breath. "I know you threw away my note. I want—"

"Stop, Melba. Just stop." Ruby scooted away from Melba. "I don't care what you want."

"I want to apologize." Melba's voice had a hollow sound to it.

"You can't. I won't let you." Now Ruby stood and faced Melba. "I don't want to hear it. You killed my chicks."

Melba's face was hidden under the brim of her hat as Ruby stood over her. Her gloved hands were folded quietly in her lap, and she gave a little shudder. Ruby felt a stab of triumph, and it carried her along on a wave of anger. "I don't care what you have to say, you can't bring them back. I don't care what you say from now on about anything! My grandpa would have come home last summer, no matter what. He always came home. Say whatever you want! Tell everybody! I'm not afraid of you anymore."

Ruby's face flushed and her throat was on fire. She leaned toward Melba, so angry she was shaking.

With her finger she jabbed Melba hard on the shoulder. "It's your turn, Melba Jane. I'm going to tell everybody in this town just what a rotten person you are, just how mean you are, how hateful. How you wanted me to believe it was my fault that my grandpa died, that your daddy died, that the whole accident happened! Maybe I'll just come to the operetta after all and tell everybody tonight! I could tell the whole town while you were standing right there on the stage with me!"

Ruby's throat had closed up, and she had to squeeze the last few words out. She stopped and took a deep breath and swallowed. "Then I'm going to tell them how my chicks died. And I'm going to make sure they know that it was all your fault. You killed them, Melba Jane. And I will never forget it."

For a moment neither girl moved and there was no sound, just the echo of Ruby's words hanging in the air above them. Then the summer noises returned, and Ruby stood up straight to collect herself. She felt light-headed. Melba kept her head down, her face still hidden by the brim of her hat.

Then she spoke. "Yes, I did." Her voice trembled. "I did. Mama says..." She didn't finish the sentence. She reached into her dress pocket and pulled out a handkerchief, then removed her gloves, pulling slowly on each finger. Ruby watched her.

"You know what I wonder about?" Melba asked. Ruby's stomach did a flutter as she saw that Melba had calluses on her palms. "I wonder if my daddy was scared that night." Melba clutched her gloves. "I wonder if he was awake. And if he was, did he think about me? I wonder about that."

Ruby wouldn't hear this, wouldn't think about this. "Go away, Melba Jane!"

Now Melba had the handkerchief in her hand, dabbing at the sweat collecting on her forehead and around her ears, dripping from the wig. Then she stood, tucked her handkerchief into her dress pocket, and walked to the opposite side of the bridge. An old pickup truck clattered over it, slowed, but did not stop. Melba stared at the lake where the sun sparkled low and golden on the water. "I miss my daddy."

A numbness spread through Ruby. She stood as still as she could, willing Melba Jane to go away.

And she did. Melba's sandals tapped across the bridge as she walked toward the schoolhouse.

23

The moon rose in a dusky blue sky. It wouldn't be dark yet for close to an hour, but in summer the eight o'clock light of evening was the best. Ruby had come home to an empty house—her mother was helping with the punch and cookies to be served after the operetta and had left Ruby a note: "Big salad in fridge! Eat up! Come watch! Love you!" Now, out in the greenhouse, Ruby read some "P" words to Bemmie, who clucked like a happy fool on her nest. She could hear faint peeping from Bemmie's one egg. Tonight would be the night, she was sure of it. It would take some time, several more hours probably, but by morning there would be a new chick.

She couldn't get Melba out of her head. She would go to the operetta. She wouldn't. Yes, she would. No, she wouldn't. No. Yes. No.

She couldn't concentrate. "Peony...people... pep...pepper...pepper-and-salt..." She sighed. "Pepper-and-salt" made her think "sweet and sour," which made her think "lemon drops," which made her think about her grandpa, which made her think about the lake and the bridge and Melba. All the fight was out of Melba—what was the matter with her? Ruby felt like she was just beginning to fight. It felt good to have the tables turned. She would go to the schoolhouse. Yes. No. She reached for Rosebud, who squawked out of her hands and hopped onto the dictionary, as if to say, *Keep reading!*

A breeze began to cool the hot day. It carried with it the sound of the Halleluia band playing in the schoolhouse. The operetta had begun. Her mama was there. The whole town was there, except her. And Miss Eula. Ruby hadn't had a letter from Miss Eula in over a week! Maybe she had decided to stay in Hawaii, after all, and was trying to find a way to tell Ruby the bad news. The thought made Ruby's stomach hurt. Oh, Miss Eula. *Write to me*, Ruby wished. She sent the wish out into the universe.

She stood up and dusted dirt and straw from her overalls and hitched up her left shoulder strap. She moved Rosebud off the dictionary and closed it. "Later, Rosie," she said. "Stay here and keep an eye on

everything. I'm going for a walk. I'll be back soon."
Ruby grabbed Miss Eula's straw hat—Dove had kept
the other one. She put it on and stared at her reflection in the window. She knew where she was going,
even if she wouldn't admit it to herself. She walked
down the porch steps and into the sultry August
night. She headed for the schoolhouse.

24

Ruby stepped through the early evening shadows, walking barefoot on a packed dirt road surrounded by wild roses and blackberry vines. Fireflies were just beginning to wink on and off. She didn't have the heart to catch one tonight. Ahead she could see the lights of the schoolhouse, like a beacon in the gathering dark.

The back door was propped open with a rock. Ruby slipped inside and crept up the backstage steps to the side-stage curtains. The chorus was singing "The Old Oaken Bucket," and Mrs. Varnado was playing the piano. Ruby peered through the curtains into the auditorium. Every seat was filled.

Ruby spotted her mother sitting with Mr. Ishee.

On the other side of Mr. Ishee was Melba Jane's mother. Her five other children were sprawled all over the aisle and hanging off seats on the edges of the rows. Ruby peeked onto the stage.

Old Ezra Jackson sat in a porch rocker, snoozing. Six more porch rockers held members of the chorus singing the end of their song. Dove was one of them. The porch was decorated with Chock full-o' Nuts coffee cans full of geraniums. Paintings were propped all over the "yard," like quilts on a line, the ugliest paintings Ruby had ever seen. Standing in front of the porch was Melba Jane. She was holding an oaken bucket, swinging it at her side and taking small, measured steps toward the front of the stage, where there was a crudely constructed well. It leaned to the right, and Ruby thought it might fall over if someone touched it. Melba wore a blue-checked dress, like Dorothy's dress in *The Wizard of Oz*. No ruby slippers. Her wig—not the same one she'd worn at the bridge—gave her a mass of wild ink-black hair that fell to her shoulders. With the wig and all the makeup she was wearing, she reminded Ruby of the Wicked Witch of the West wearing the wrong clothes.

As the chorus finished singing and Melba walked

to the front of the stage, she passed underneath a papier-mâché and construction-paper apple tree. The branches were laden with bright red apples that were fixed onto the branches with chicken wire. Melba was smiling—no, she was beaming. Ruby could see how being onstage, in front of her public, restored Melba, made her happier than just about anything, made her forget her troubles. It was how Ruby felt when she was with Miss Eula…happier than just about anything.

Melba began her soliloquy. She spoke in a voice loud enough to peel paint. "How *dear* to my heart— *dear dear dear* to my heart—are the scenes of my childhood! Oh! How *dear!*"

"Oh, how putrid." Ruby didn't know if she could watch.

As Melba approached the well, she passed under the last branch of the apple tree. She hung the bucket on a peg at the well. She held out her arms, stood on her tiptoes, and did two complete whirl-arounds. She was about to sing.

But she never sang. A piece of chicken wire snagged at her long black wig. Melba kept whirling. The wire kept snagging. Apples fell to the stage, *plop! plop! plop!*—and as Melba Jane stopped her whirl, the apple tree wore a shiny black wig and Melba Jane Latham stood on the schoolhouse stage in front of the town of Halleluia, little wisps of hair on a bluish scalp, practically bald.

25

The audience gasped.

Ruby blinked. "Good garden of peas."

The wig dangled from the branch in the spotlight, several feet behind Melba Jane. All eyes were on the wig. On Melba. The wig. Even the chorus was speechless.

The only person who didn't notice what was happening was Mrs. Varnado, who was now plunking "Country Gardens" lightly on the piano, swaying back and forth, waiting for Melba Jane to start her soliloquy and then sing.

Ruby saw the look on Melba's face.... She was terrified. She was struggling to stay onstage, to stay standing. Ruby held her breath as Melba opened her mouth.

"As I was saying." Melba's voice was tiny. Her

hands trembled. But, actress that Melba so fiercely wanted to be, she did not move from her spot. "How dear to my heart are the scenes of my childhood!" Ruby thought she might be rallying. "I remember the days when…" She faltered. Her eyes filled with tears. She stood there. Motionless. No one spoke.

She'd forgotten her lines! Ruby licked her lips. Out in the audience, Melba's mother rose to her feet.

Melba began again but went in another direction. "I remember when my daddy…" Her voice was a croak.

A chill raced up Ruby's spine and across her shoulders. Without thinking, she strode out to Melba, taking giant steps. Melba jumped and stared at Ruby. Her eyes were as wide as half-dollars, and she was struck dumb. Not a word would come from her mouth. Ruby realized, with a crazy rush of bravado, that she was standing in front of the entire town of Halleluia, Mississippi, next to Melba Jane Latham, who was practically bald and totally mute. She glanced at Dove, sitting in a porch rocker with her mouth open.

Ruby turned to Melba Jane. The two girls' eyes met and they stared at each other. Ruby took a deep breath. "Your father!" she said. She gave Melba a say-something! look.

Melba's mother began walking toward the stage, but Ruby's mother reached for her. She put her hand gently on Leila Latham's arm as if to say, *Wait...*

Melba found her voice but not her lines. "My father?..." Her face crumbled.

"Yes," Ruby said slowly. "Yes, I remember him *so* well!" Melba blinked. *How? How did Ruby remember him?* She said the first thing that came to her. "He taught you...he taught you all the constellations, right?" Melba's mouth dropped open. Ruby's face flushed. "Did he teach you the firefly poem? My grandpa taught me that poem." Ruby took off Miss Eula's hat and in one smooth motion put it over Melba Jane's slightly blue head.

"Let's see if I can remember it." Ruby held out her hands and cupped in them an imaginary firefly. Then she held her cupped hands in front of her and recited the rhyme her grandfather had taught her long ago:

"Oh, Little One, Bright One,"

she said, in a clear, ringing voice.

"You are the first one, so you are the light.
You are the one we follow tonight.
Fly away now to your free life—so sweet!

We'll follow you with our true hearts till we meet
on the side of the shore, in the meadow so fair,
in the place where our souls soar into the air..."

Ruby parted her palms and lifted them upward. She imagined she could see a real firefly winking and flying into the darkening sky. She pointed in that direction. "Look! There's another one! Catch it quick, for good luck!" Ruby opened her eyes wide at Melba. "Go on," she said, her teeth clenched. "Grab it."

And Melba did. "I've got one!" she croaked, cupping her hands.

"*Every*body find a firefly!" shouted Ruby. They did. The audience was on its feet, arms outstretched, and the chorus rushed to the front of the stage with Ruby and Melba Jane. They began crazily jumping and catching imaginary fireflies and holding them in their cupped hands. Ruby had no idea what to do next.

Mrs. Varnado, who had been prepared to play all of "Country Gardens," began playing "Glow, Little Glow-Worm." Melba, who had recovered herself some, let her imaginary glowworm/firefly go into the night, and so did the audience. Ruby hooked her arm in Melba's and danced her off the stage. Melba let herself be escorted. She left the wig where it was. Tot and Cleebo Wilson pulled the curtain closed. "Take a bow, everybody," said Tot. "Bless your hearts." The curtains opened again.

The auditorium erupted in applause.

26

Melba and Ruby stood backstage in the darkness, and Ruby began to feel awkward. It had all happened so fast. She shoved her hands in her overalls pockets. "They loved us."

Melba opened her mouth, closed it, and opened it again. "Thanks."

The applause continued. Ruby pulled her hands out of her pockets. "They want you to take a bow."

Melba blinked back tears. "Want to come?"

Ruby shook her head. "I'm going home."

The audience called for Ruby and Melba. Ruby walked to the back door.

"Ruby, wait!"

"What?" Ruby turned her head and hitched up her left overalls strap.

Melba put a hand on her forehead and held it there. "I'm sorry about your chicks." Two tears rolled down her face.

Ruby's heart began a *thump-thump* in her chest. She pushed open the back door.

Melba took a step toward Ruby. "It was an accident." She wiped at her eyes.

Ruby stood half in, half out of the doorway. She listened to her heart as it thumped in her chest, *just-wait, just-wait*. She pulled at her earlobe and felt her pulse beating in her temples.

Melba wiped her nose with the back of her hand. "I'm really so sorry, Ruby."

Ruby's shoulders fell and she took a slow breath. "I know it was an accident," she said.

Melba sniffed. "Yes."

Ruby chewed her lip and looked at Melba. "I'm sorry about your daddy."

Melba wiped at her eyes. "I'm sorry about your grandpa."

Ruby thought a moment, then pushed her hair away from her face. "...And about your hair. And your blue head."

Melba blinked. Ruby shrugged.

Aunt Tot stuck her head through the side-stage

curtains. "Hurry up, you two! Bless your hearts! Your public wants to bestow accolades upon you!" She popped her head back on the other side of the curtain. "Hold your ponies! They're still here, and they are *coming*!"

"I'll bring the hat back to you tomorrow," said Melba.

"Okay."

"I don't want to stay and visit."

"I don't want you to."

And with that, Ruby left Melba and the schoolhouse and stepped into the soft summer night. Rosebud was standing outside the door. "Rosebud! How did you get out?" Ruby picked her up and stroked her feathers. "Let's take a walk, girl."

She walked to town, taking her time. Rosebud clucked and strutted behind her in the moonlit dark, stopping to investigate every bug and bit of dust. Ruby waited for her. She gazed up at the starry sky. "We're under this same sky, Miss Eula, no matter where we are. I remember." Soon she was walking down her sandy lane behind the closed-up mercantile and the bank and the post office. There was the silver maple tree that was Miss Eula and Ruby's post office. It threw long shimmery shadows across the lane. She gave it a pat. It would be a long, long letter she'd have to write, to tell Miss Eula all that had happened on this day.

Rosebud squawked and Ruby bent down to pick her up. As she did, she saw something. There was a note in the knothole. Mail. It was pink.

August 1

Dear Ruby Darlin',

I got off the bus from Jackson, and there wasn't a soul in town—they were all at the operetta! So I bustled myself over there and watched from the shadows. I saw what you did for Melba. Ruby, I am proud to know you.

If you have missed me half as much as I've missed you, I hope you'll come straight to the Pink Palace when you get this note. I am parching some peanuts and laying out 732 photographs to be put in photo albums. Isn't THAT a lucky number. It's the luckiest number yet.

I have stories to tell! Bring Dove. Tell Melba to bring me my hat, and I'll trade her a pair of flip-flops. I got flip-flops for everybody! Miss Mattie is going to get a shipment of 400 pairs of flip-flops next week! Won't she be thrilled! I know I'm thrilled to be home. Hurry and come see me!

Love,
your (still) favorite grandmother,
Miss Eula

27

Ruby sat down with a thud. Suddenly her heart felt too large for her chest, like someone had pulled a plug and *whoosh!*—her heart had expanded, filled with…something. The feeling rose up her neck and stung the back of her throat—tears! She slapped her hand to her chest and tried a calm breath, but it didn't work—her feelings swept over her like a wave, and one sob turned into two, and three, and then the dam broke and Ruby just let it come.

Tears made puddles all over the pink note, and Ruby cried until she had no tears left. Rosebud squatted a few inches away from Ruby and eyed her. Ruby wiped her nose with her shirtsleeve and reached for Rosebud to hug her. The chicken squawked and freed herself. She strutted a few feet away, settled again, and clucked, watching Ruby.

"Silly chicken." Ruby hiccuped. "You follow me everywhere! I *told* you I was coming back." She laughed at her own joke, and her laughter hitched in her throat.

She wiped her eyes with the palms of her hands. She shuddered all over and took a deep breath. She folded the note and shoved it into her front overalls pocket. "Miss Eula's *home*." A sweet feeling spread warmly from Ruby's heart, down her arms, into her fingertips.

"Life does go on, Rosebud," she whispered. She brushed her wild red hair out of her face. "I mean, look at you. I rescued your mother and now here you are, watching me cry." She giggled at a new thought. "You're a pretty good friend...for a *chicken*."

She scooped up her friend and squeezed her tight. Rosebud screeched and Ruby laughed and released her. "Let's go, girl!" she shouted. Then she ran, Rosebud scrabbling behind her. She ran along the lane, over the bridge, up the hill, and on toward the Pink Palace.

A Reading Group Guide

(Especially for grandmothers and granddaughters
inspired by Ruby and Miss Eula, Chicken Libera-
tors of the Highest Order)

Questions to *Cluck* About

1. Grandpa Garnet told Ruby that people are like lemon
   drops, "sour and sweet together." What did he mean?
   What is sour and sweet about Ruby? Miss Eula?
   Melba Jane?

2. Miss Eula is known for the motto Life does go on.
   What do you think she means?

3. Ruby and Melba Jane each experience the loss of a
   loved one, but each of them deals with that loss
   differently. How does Ruby handle it? Melba Jane?
   In what ways could they have helped each other?
   Who helps you when you are sad?

4. Miss Mattie comforts Ruby by telling her, "This
   family is full of strong women who know how to
   laugh." Explain how humor helps Ruby and Miss
   Eula deal with their sadness. How have you used
   humor to help you get through tough times?

5. "We're all different and we're all the same." Or at least, that's what Dove says. How are Ruby and Melba Jane different from each other? How are they alike? What can they learn from each other? In what ways did the attack on the chickens change Ruby and Melba Jane?

6. Both Ruby and Melba Jane become friends with Dove. How can differences in interests and personalities strengthen friendships? In what ways can new friends affect old friendships? Do any of the friendships in *Love, Ruby Lavender* make you see your own friendships differently?

7. Both Melba Jane and Ruby hold grudges against each other. What are the dangers of grudges? Have you ever had a conflict with a friend? What did you do in that situation? Would you handle it differently now?

8. Ruby looks to Miss Eula for comfort, security, and love. Why does Ruby send her grandmother chicken updates even though she thinks Miss Eula has abandoned her for some new (smelly!) baby? Has Miss Eula really abandoned Ruby?

Things To Do

1. Ruby drew a map of Halleluia. She included the silver maple tree and the spot where she and Miss Eula saved Ivy, Bemmie, and Bess. Why has Ruby drawn these places on her map? Draw a map of your own town or neighborhood. What special landmarks would you include? Why?

2. The responses Ruby writes on Mr. Ishee's questionnaire reveal a lot about her. On a piece of paper, write your own responses to the questionnaire, as if Mr. Ishee had sent it to you. Share your answers with the group. Discuss one new thing you learned about someone in your group.

3. Ruby gives a lot of free advice. What advice would you offer someone about getting along with friends?

4. Ruby and Miss Eula have their own secret mailbox, and they send letters between Hawaii and Halleluia instead of phoning each other. Why is letter writing so important to them? Send a letter to someone older than you—to a relative, a family friend, or a neighbor. What will you tell them? What will you ask that person? What might you send along with your letter?

5. Imagine this was Melba Jane's story instead of Ruby's. How might Melba describe Ruby? What would she reveal about her own feelings? Write a letter that Melba Jane might send to her own grandmother.

Mr. Ishee's Fourth Grade
September Something (I forget, exactly)
Author Interview: Deborah Wiles
By: Ruby Garnet Lavender (against her will)

Pee Ess to Mr. Ishee: I protest. Is the whole entire YEAR going to be like this? Project after project? Mama tells me I have to do this assignment. She says I will learn a lot. I think I will learn that chickens are more interesting than authors. Still, I think this author wrote a pretty good book, for a grown-up. So here is my project.

Ruby Lavender (RGL): Hello, Deborah Wiles. I have chosen you for my author interview school project. The problem is, I can't find information about you in the library, so I am wondering if this means you are not too interesting. (You would fit right in, here in Halleluia, Mississippi.) Maybe I should have chosen someone else. . . .

Deborah Wiles (DW): Hi, Ruby! I'm glad you chose me. I'm sorry you haven't been able to find much information. That's because Love, Ruby Lavender is my first novel. I am a new author, but I have been writing and telling my story for many years. <u>Ruby</u> is part of my story.

RGL: YOUR story? I thought it was MY story!

DW: It's your story, of course. But what happens to you and Miss Eula and Melba Jane and Dove is made up. The details are real—they come from my life and are part of my story.

RGL: How is that? I mean, you don't live in the Pink Palace, and you don't have a chicken named Bemmie . . . do you? If you do, check for blue feet. Bemmie is always running off—I'll bet you've got my chicken! Wait, let me go check the chicken house. . . .

DW: No, no, I don't have a chicken, but I had a wacky grandmother named Eula, and she lived in a little Mississippi town, and I visited her there every summer. There was a town store, owned by Mr. Jeff, who always gave me lemon drops. My aunt Mitt had a beautiful flower garden, and my great-grandmother, Nanny, had the world's most fabulous vegetable garden. The postmistress really <u>was</u> named Dot. And . . . I had great-great aunts named Bess and Bemmie!

RGL: You turned your AUNTS into CHICKENS?

DW: Yes! They were very old when I knew them and I thought they looked like chickens! You can take any detail of your life and put it into your stories.

RGL: I wonder if Miss Mattie would make a good chicken. What other details of your life did you put into <u>Love, Ruby Lavender</u>? Did <u>your</u> Miss Eula really go to Hawaii?

DW: Yes, she did. I lived in Hawaii when my dad was stationed there in the Air Force, and my grandmother came to visit us when my baby sister was born. The sugar-sand beach and the volcano that Miss Eula talks about in her letters—I remember them well. I also remember laughing a lot with my grandmother, so I wrote about that, too.

RGL: I love how Miss Eula and Ruby (that's me) laugh together and love each other so much.

DW: Me, too. My grandmother loved me just like
       Miss Eula loves you, so I know what that love
       feels like. And I know what it feels like to
       love someone fiercely, and to be so angry
       you could hurt someone, to be sad, disap-
       pointed, forgiven . . . I write about feelings
       a lot—they are important to me.

RGL: I'd rather read about root beer floats! Mr.
       Ishee makes the best root beer floats—fizzy
       and smooth and cold—just right. I want one
       now!

DW: Mmmmm . . . me, too. Remember how hot it
       was the day Mr. Ishee made those floats?
       And remember the rainstorm that swirled
       the dust everywhere? I try to use all my
       senses when I write. I ask myself, What did
       my world sound like, smell like, feel like,
       look like, taste like? All the food in Love,
       Ruby Lavender is food I loved as a child, all
       the—

RGL: Zucchini? You loved zucchini? Excuse me,
       but you were a strange child.

DW: Probably! I was an observer, too, like Dove. I
      listened to people, and I paid attention to
      small details. The black-eyed Susans, the
      zucchini, the beans in Miss Mattie's store,
      the way the bees buzz around the honey-
      suckle . . . I remember vividly all the details
      of growing up in a small Southern town, and
      I wanted to capture those details on paper.
      Details make your story special.

RGL: Well, I don't think there is anything special
      about zucchini, or the dusty floor in Miss
      Mattie's store—the floor I have to sweep, by
      the way. I do like writing letters, though.
      There are lots of letters in <u>Love, Ruby
      Lavender</u>.

DW: I think you can tell your story in letters, too.
      It's another way to let someone know about
      you. Ruby (that's you) reveals a lot about her
      world through her letters, don't you think?

RGL: I sure do. I am not called a blabbermouth
      for nothin'.

DW: I didn't know you were called a blabber-
      mouth! That's news to me.

RGL: I can also tell you the name of Bemmie's new chick, if you want to know it.

DW: I would love to know! Tell me.

RGL: The new chick is a HE. A rooster, named Elvis.

DW: Elvis! What a great name!

RGL: I have good naming skills. And good free advice. Like right now I can tell you that if I were you, I would have made sure that Ruby didn't have to do an author interview for a school project. I would have her go fishing instead.

DW: Would you rather be fishing right now?

RGL: I'd rather be doing just about anything else right now.

DW: Well, I'm ready to go, if you've got all the information you need for your project. It's been fun visiting with you for a few minutes. I hope we can do it again sometime.

RGL: Come to the Pink Palace after work—you can meet Elvis. He is red-feathered and musically talented. He screeches in all keys, day and night. He crows right through my dictionary reading. Rosebud runs in circles around him and swoons. Miss Eula says Elvis has got to stop "being so enthusiastic" or she's gonna have to think about eating chicken again.

DW: She's kidding, right?

RGL: Right. But it's a good STORY, isn't it? Good garden of peas! Did you see that?

DW: What?

RGL: That was Bemmie! And Herman! Look at them, running off! I've got to go! Thanks for the interview!

Look for the next hilarious and heartfelt coming-of-age novel by Deborah Wiles:

Each LITTLE BIRD That SINGS

Ten-year-old Comfort Snowberger has attended 247 funerals. But that's not surprising, considering that her family runs the town funeral home. And even though Great-uncle Edisto keeled over with a heart attack and Great-great-aunt Florentine dropped dead—just like that—six months later, Comfort knows how to deal with loss, or so she thinks. She's more concerned with avoiding her crazy cousin Peach and trying to figure out why her best friend, Declaration, suddenly won't talk to her. Life is full of surprises. And the biggest one of all is learning what it takes to handle them.

Turn the page to read the first chapter of this extraordinary new book!

CHAPTER I

I come from a family with a lot of dead people.

Great-uncle Edisto keeled over with a stroke on a Saturday morning after breakfast last March. Six months later, Great-great-aunt Florentine died—just like that—in the vegetable garden. And, of course, there are all the dead people who rest temporarily downstairs, until they go off to the Snapfinger Cemetery. I'm related to them, too, Uncle Edisto always told me, "Everybody's kin, Comfort," he said.

Downstairs at Snowberger's, my daddy deals with death by misadventure, illness, and natural causes galore. Sometimes I ask him how somebody died. He tells me, then he says, "It's not how you die that makes the important impression, Comfort; it's how you *live*. Now go live awhile, honey, and let me get back to work." But I'm getting ahead of myself. Let me back up. I'll start with Great-uncle Edisto and last March, since that death involves me—I witnessed it.

It was March 27, the first day of Easter vacation. I had just finished deviling eggs in the upstairs kitchen. Uncle Edisto and I were planning the first picnic of spring. My best friend, Declaration Johnson, would be joining us. I was sitting at the kitchen table, scarfing down my Chocolate Buzz Krispies. Uncle Edisto licked the end of his pencil and scribbled onto the crossword puzzle in the *Aurora County News*. Daddy and Mama were working. Great-great-aunt Florentine had just sneaked her ritual piece of bacon from the paper-toweled rack by the stove.

"I'm off to the garden, darlin's!" she said. "I feel a need to sing to the peas!" She kissed Great-uncle Edisto's head. He looked up from his crossword puzzle and sang—to the tune of "Oh! Susanna"—"Oh, Peas-Anna! Don't you cry for me . . ." I laughed with my mouth full of cereal. Aunt Florentine blew me a kiss, then she drifted out of the room, singing to herself: "For I come from Mississippi with a Moon Pie on my knee!"

"'Moon Pie'!" said Uncle Edisto, poising his pencil over the crossword puzzle. "That's it! Twenty-four across!"

The sky had been clouding up all morning, but I was ignoring all signs of rain. A grumble of thunder brought my dog, Dismay, to the kitchen, where he shoved himself at my feet under the table, pressed his shaggy black body against my legs, and shuddered.

"Oh, now, doggie!" said Great-uncle Edisto, peering under the table at Dismay. "You don't have to worry about no thunder! It's a beautiful day for a pic-a-nic!" Uncle Edisto was always optimistic. "Yessir," he said, smiling at me, "a pic-a-nic at Listening Rock should be just about perfect today!"

Then—*Craaaack!* went the thunder. *Sizzle!* went the lightning. And *Boom!* . . . The sky opened wide and rain sheared down like curtains.

Dismay scrambled for my lap, bobbling the kitchen table on his back.

"Whoa, doggie!" called Great-uncle Edisto. He steadied the table as Dismay yelped and tried to get out from *under* the table and *onto* me.

"Down, Dismay!" I shouted. Milk sloshed out of my bowl, and I made a mighty *push-back* in my chair. Dismay's toenails clawed my legs and his thick coat crammed itself into my nose as my chair tipped sideways with me and Dismay in it. *"Umpgh!"* The air left my body. My Snowberger's baseball cap popped right off my head. And there I was, lying on the kitchen floor with a sixty-five-pound dog in my face. He stuck his shaggy snout into my neck and shivered. An obituary headline flashed into my mind: *Local Girl, 10, Done In by Storm and Petrified Pet!*

Into the middle of all this commotion clomped my little sister, Merry, wearing Mama's high heels and a red slip that pooled around her feet. I peeked at her from under my dog blanket. As soon as she saw me, her eyebrows popped high and her mouth rounded into a tiny O of surprise.

"Dead!" she said.

"No," I said. I spit out dog hair. It was fine and silky and tasted like the cow pond.

"You all right, Comfort?" Great-uncle Edisto towered over me. He wore fat blue suspenders, and I could smell his old-person-after-shaving smell.

"I'm okay."

My head hurt. My plans were ruined. My dog was overwrought. But other than that, I was fine.

"Fumfort!" chirped Merry.

"Move, Dismay!" I pushed at him, but Dismay was

glued to me like Elmer's. He gave my face three quick licks with his wet tongue, as if to say, *Yep, it's thunder! Yep, it's thunder!! Yep, it's thunder!!!*

Merry turned herself around and stomped out of the kitchen, singing, to the tune of "Jingle Bells": "Fumfort dead, Fumfort dead, Fumfort dead away!"

Downstairs the front doors slammed, and my older brother, Tidings, who had been painting the fence by the front parking lot, yelled, "Attention, all personnel! Where are the *big* umbrellas! I need rain cover!"

Dismay immediately detached himself from me and scuttled for the grand front staircase to find Tidings, who was bigger than I was and who offered more protection.

I gazed at the ceiling and took stock of the situation. One: It was raining hard. There went my picnic. Two: Best friend or not, Declaration would not come over in the rain—she didn't like to get wet. There went my plans. Three: I didn't have a three, but if I thought about it long enough, I would.

Great-uncle Edisto extended a knobby hand to me and winced as he pulled me to my feet. He gave me my baseball cap, and I used both hands to pull it back onto my head.

"You're gettin' to be a big girl," he said. He picked

up the newspaper, tucked his pencil behind his ear, and looked out at the downpour. His voice took on a thoughtful tone. "The rain serves us."

Great-uncle Edisto always talked like that. Everything, even death, served us, according to him. Everything had a grand purpose, and there was nothing amiss in the universe; it was our job to adjust to whatever came our way. I didn't get it.

"We can have us some deviled eggs and tuner-fish sandwiches right here in the kitchen, Comfort," he went on. "Or, we can try another day for that pic-a-nic."

When I didn't answer, he turned his head to find me. "What's the matter, honey?"

"I'm disappointed." I studied my scratched-up legs.

"So am I!" Great-uncle Edisto took a Snowberger's handkerchief out of his shirt pocket and mopped at his face. "I like to pic-a-nic more than a bee likes to bumble!"

He did.

While we straightened the table and chairs and cleaned up the spilled cereal, Great-uncle Edisto told me about how disappointments can be good things—like the time he thought he'd planted Abraham Lincoln tomato plants in the garden but found out later they were really Sunsweet cherry tomatoes. He'd had his heart set on sinking his teeth into those fat Abe Lincoln tomatoes, but then he discovered that he liked the Sunsweets even better—and besides, he could pop a whole Sunsweet into his mouth at once and save his front teeth some wear and tear. "A distinct advantage at my age," he said.

"That doesn't help my mood," I said. The rain pounded so hard on the tin roof, it made a roaring sound inside the kitchen and we had to shout to be heard.

"Think of disappointment as a happy little surprise, Comfort. For instance . . ." Great-uncle Edisto pushed his glasses up on his nose and smiled like he had just invented a new thought. "I think I'll get me a nap." He was breathing hard. "There's always something good to come out of disappointment, Comfort. You'll see."

I could tell by the rhythm and tone of his voice that he was working up to his grand finale: "Open your arms to life! Let it strut into your heart in all its messy glory!"

"I don't like messes," I told him. "I like my plans."

Uncle Edisto patted me on the shoulder and lumbered off to his room. I called Declaration on the kitchen telephone, but her line was busy. I hung up and waited for her to call me, but she didn't, so I tried dialing her six more times. Then I gave up.

Tidings slammed the downstairs doors on his way back outside, and Dismay came to find me. We went to my closet to wait for something good to happen. I do my best thinking in the closet. It's quiet and comfortable and smells like opportunity. I sat with my back against the wall and my knees under my chin. Dismay sat facing me (it's a big closet), with his paws touching my bare toes. He panted nervously and his dog saliva drip-drip-dripped onto my feet.

"Thunder's gone," I said. "You can rest easy, boy."

Dismay wasn't sure, but he smiled at me anyway, with those shiny dog eyes. It made me want to hug him, so I did. His tail *thump-thump-thump*ed the floor.

The next thing I knew, Great-uncle Edisto surprised us all.

Great-great-aunt Florentine whooped for everyone to come. (Her bedroom was next to Great-uncle Edisto's bedroom, and she was standing at her mirror, she said later, soaking wet, untying the ribbon on her sunbonnet, when Great-uncle Edisto took his tumble.)

"It's an apoplexy!" she hollered. "Stroke!"

Everyone came running. We picked up Uncle

Edisto from where he had landed, put him into bed, covered him with one of Aunt Florentine's lavender-scented quilts, and called Doc MacRee. Mama sat on one side of Uncle Edisto's bed. She held Merry on her lap and looked exquisitely sad. Daddy kneeled next to Uncle Edisto on the other side of the bed and stroked his pale forehead. Tidings stood at attention next to Daddy, with his hand over his heart and a devastated look on his face.

Great-uncle Edisto gazed at us peacefully. He took us all in, like he was seeing us new, for the first time. His face was soft (turning a little gray), and, with the covers tucked under his chin, he looked for all the world like a small boy.

"Time to go home," he whispered. He blinked a slow blink, and when he opened his eyes, he seemed to be looking beyond us, to a land we couldn't see . . . a new world to explore.

"You *are* home, Uncle Edisto," I said. My heart pounded against my chest in a *Don't go! Don't go! Don't go!* beat. I kept one hand on Dismay; my dog stood next to me, calm and silent, keeping watch.

"You go on, Edisto," said Great-great-aunt Florentine, tears streaming down her wrinkled face. "It's your time. Have a wonderful trip, darlin'." She kissed him on the forehead and he closed his eyes. Then he smiled and . . . off he went.

I cried into Aunt Florentine's wet bosom. Everybody cried, because death is hard. Death is sad. But death is part of life. When someone you know dies, it's your job to keep on living.

So . . . we did. We adjusted. We did what we always do when death comes calling:

We gathered together.

We started cooking.

We called the relatives.

We called our friends.

We did not have to call the funeral home.

We *are* the funeral home.

I wrote the obituary.